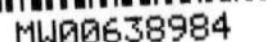

CANNON
BOOKS

THANK YOU KIM, MY ROCK DURING THE STORM OF CREATIVITY

I'M GRATEFUL TO
SUSAN TEPPER
GER BURKE
MEG TUITE
BRUCE RETTIG
FOR REVIEWING AND COMMENTING ON MY WORDS.
THANK YOU FOR YOUR THOUGHTFULNESS.

CANNON BOOKS

THE MADNESS OF BEING

STORIES

BY

RON D'ALENA

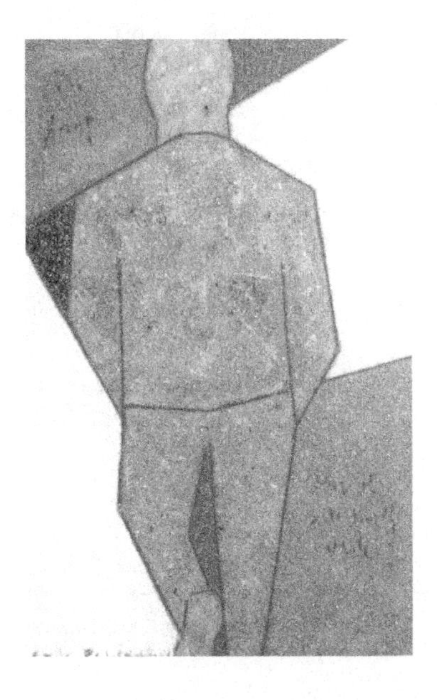

MEDFORD, OREGON

MMXXI

Cannon Books LLC

The Madness of Being

Stories

First Edition September 2021

Published by Cannon Books

Front cover Art

"Was it all worthwhile?" 1997, oil on canvas (58x60cm), Erik Pevernagie (b. 1939)

To view this painting, please see commons.wikimedia.org/wiki/File:Was_it_all_worth_while.jpg

Author photograph: Kim Kisling

Portions of this book originally appeared in the following publications:

Crannóg Magazine; EDGE; Bacopa Literary Review; Big Lucks; Johnny America; Connotation Press Online; Blue Crow Magazine; Conclave: A Journal of Character

Contents

THE MADNESS OF BEING

STORIES

Bonnie, Troy and Tommie

Bonnie Leonard put the envelope next to the ashtray on the kitchen table. She felt like screaming. Instead, she popped a Vicodin, washed it down with a sip of wine, lit a cigarette and went into the kitchen. Sitting on the Formica countertop next to the sink, she glanced out the window at the empty driveway. Soon Troy would be home from work and when he found out he would be plenty mad.

Troy pulled his Camaro up to the garage and stopped. He opened the car door and got out slow. His right arm cradled a paper grocery sack. He was beginning to let himself go—unshaven, overdue for a haircut. Bonnie watched him step over the garden hose and come up the concrete walkway. He wobbled a little and she could tell he'd stopped off for a couple beers after work.

The front door creaked open and as soon as Troy entered the house Bonnie said, "Well, it finally came."

"Huh?" He ran his fingers through his hair and brushed off some drywall dust from his shoulders.

"The notice. It finally came."

He sat down at the kitchen table. Without picking up the envelope, he looked at the big red words under his address:

IMPORTANT: OPEN IMMEDIATELY.

His eyes held no curiosity, betrayed no feeling. Bonnie supposed the anger he had been venting during the past months was now gone, used up as their world changed into something unrecognizable. First, her job in accounts payable at Eric's Auto Parts & Accessories had disappeared after nearly six years. Then Troy had been told his drywalling job at the Winchester Motel was over at the end of the month.

Troy pulled a Miller out of the sack and twisted it open. Bonnie went to the fridge and got last night's Chinese take-out. She dumped the Kung Pao chicken and rice into a Tupperware bowl and put it in the microwave.

"What about the kids," she said, "what are we going to tell the kids?"

"They're grown up. They're capable of understanding grown up problems."

"But they grew up in this house."

"Look, it's just a house."

The microwave beeped. Bonnie looked at the food, buried her index finger in the middle of it all.

"Still a little cold," she said. She reset the microwave and went back to sitting on the countertop by the sink. She gathered up her freshly washed brown hair in both hands and then let it fall to the small of her back. She said, "Gary and Dee called on the telephone. They want to know if we want to meet them at DeLux Billiards later on. They're already there and said we could meet them if we wanted."

Troy got up from the chair. The kitchen floor creaked under the linoleum as he walked over to the sink. He sipped his beer and leaned against Bonnie. He stood there, looking out through the window, looking across Haven Avenue at Gary and Dee's house. Gary and Dee had recently moved to San Jose from L.A. They had bought their house from the Hempel family as a quick sale for the amount of the bank loan.

Bonnie took the cigarette from her mouth and looked at her watch. She said, "So you want to go to DeLux or not?"

Troy said, "Would you look at that."

She knew what he was talking about: Gary and Dee's roof, newly done in Spanish tiles, the only tiled roof on the block.

The microwave beeped. They ignored it.

He said, "Christ, Bonnie, I thought things would work out by themselves. You know, hard work, put in the hours and things would work out. I might be crazy, but I still don't know how all this happened. I don't know when the trouble started. I can't explain it."

As he talked, he avoided her eyes. He looked at the floor, the toaster, the microwave, anything but her.

He continued, "I'm ashamed this whole thing didn't work out. What a load of crap. It's hard to take such crap."

Bonnie dropped her cigarette butt into the sink and grabbed the soft pack lying next to the coffee pot. Empty. No more smokes. She took another sip of wine and began swinging her legs back and forth, letting her shoeless heels thump gently against the cabinet below the sink.

Outside, the sun glinted above the western foothills, making bloodshot patterns against the clouds. Gradually the afterglow faded and everything became gray.

Troy turned from the window and looked at the microwave. Then he looked back to Bonnie. He said, "Hey, when's that damn food going to be ready, anyway?"

FORTY MINUTES LATER, they pulled into a spot between a pickup and Gary and Dee's urine-colored Hummer. Three months ago, parking had spilled into the vacant lot across the street. Now there was room enough to park a dozen semitrailers. Troy turned off the motor and sat motionless in the dark, staring past the dirty windshield, staring at the neon lettering fastened to the side of the brick building:

DELUX BILLARDS.

Bonnie Leonard waited quietly. She folded her arms across her tummy and remembered how much weight she'd gained with the first one—the one that didn't make it. Her tummy had been watermelon-big when the moving company delivered all their old furniture and some boxes from the downtown apartment. Sitting on the floor of their new garage, eating pepperoni pizza, how could they have ever known about the bad things?

A distant siren brought Bonnie back. She leaned over and kissed her husband's stubbled cheek.

He said, "Do you realize our private life is going to be public?"

A vision came to Bonnie of a FOR SALE sign planted next to the row of junipers in the front lawn. With a voice muffled with emotion she said, "It's not too late to change your mind. If you want, we can turn around and go home."

"Home?" he said. "What home?"

They walked across the parking lot and into the place. The juke was going loud, pushing Mick Jagger's voice through the big speakers hanging from the ceiling. Only three of the nine tables were in play. Immediately they saw Gary and Dee at one of the tables. Gary was standing there, drinking a pint, wearing the camouflage jacket he'd bought a few months back. Dee was leaning over the cushioned table edge, trying a difficult bank shot—yellow #1, side pocket. A rectangular light hung low and in its glow Dee's face looked slightly bent to the left—an injury, she had said, courtesy of her last husband. Dee sunk the shot and her cue rolled into position to tap green #6 into the left corner pocket.

At the table, Bonnie and Dee hugged and patted each other on the back while their husbands shook hands. Gary was six-two, a few inches taller than Troy. Gary motioned to the waitress. He ordered a pitcher of Bud Light for the four of them and a double platter of hot wings—ranch on the side.

"Now," said Gary, "how about the two of us against you two?"

Troy turned to Bonnie. Annoyance flickered across his face. He said, "Okay, baby, get ready to kick some insurance broker butt all over this damn place."

Bonnie forced a smile and nervously tucked the loose edges of her blue and white checkered blouse into her high-waisted jeans.

Dee said, "Good Heavens, all you boys are alike with your competitive nonsense."

Troy jammed four quarters into the slot on the side of the pool table and began racking the balls.

Gary laughed. "Come on, Dee, you know deep down inside we're no different from Neanderthals."

He zipped his camo jacket to his chin, zipped it back down, zipped it back up again. Then he started going on and on about his hunting expedition. That's what he called his vacation four months ago to that private ranch in Texas—a hunting expedition. The owner of the ranch had imported two dozen Thompson Gazelles from Tanzania and sold hunting permits to anyone willing to pay the high price. Gary went through every detail of the big day: the trek on foot across acres and acres of farmland, the downed Tommie ram with a busted heart, the champagne dinner right there in the field—summer light falling beneath the flat horizon, ranch hands preparing the antelope for trophy mounting.

When he finished racking the balls, Troy chalked his stick, and then stood there jingling the change in his pocket as Gary continued to talk.

Gary said, "We're thinking about painting our house. Avocado green isn't working against the new Spanish tiles. Dee thinks we should change the color to beige, or something along those lines. You know, sort of give things a Spanish villa feel. What do you guys think?"

Troy was staring at the floor, still jingling the change in his pocket. "Prick," he mumbled.

"What's that?" Gary asked.

Troy's mouth opened and shut a few times then he regained his composure. "Hell," he said, "I know what I think. I think it's time to play some 8 Ball."

Bonnie smiled and snuck a Vicodin into her mouth and washed it down with a sip of Bud Light.

THE QUARTER MOON shone silver-blue in the darkness above the power lines. Troy buckled his seatbelt, started the motor and swung his Camaro onto the road. They drove in silence, and whenever they neared their neighborhood he veered away, headed in a different direction.

Now they were going west down Almaden Expressway. Maple and crape myrtle trees lined the road. Leaves tugged from their branches by the September breeze spiraled around and around everywhere. Finally, Troy turned left into the Alamitos Creek Mall, a small strip of seven buildings. He drove through the vacant parking lot, went around to the back. He drove down a narrow alleyway separating rear store entrances from a wooden fence edging a block of single story homes crowned with obsolete television antennas. He drove up to the door of Gary's insurance business. Then he stopped.

Bonnie said, "Troy, what in God's name are we doing here?"

Troy ignored her, got out of the car, flipped his cigarette onto the ground. Dried leaves rustled against the wooden fence. Amber lights along the edge of the alley made Troy's shadow move against the concrete building as he got a crowbar from the trunk. He took the bar to the rear entrance of Gary's office and fitted it into the crack between door and frame. He pulled and Bonnie jumped in her seat, startled by the staccato of cracking wood. He pulled a second time and the door swung outward.

Bonnie opened the passenger door and hurried over to him.

"Troy, let's just go home, go home and get into bed. Would you like that? Us getting into bed early—no TV, just us in bed."

Troy's voice was harsh. "Listen, don't you go touching anything in here. Let me do the touching."

He entered the insurance office and Bonnie padded after him. The place smelled like disinfectant: carpet or toilet bowl cleaner, something harsh. Parking lot lights filtered in through the plate glass window at the front of the office, making things visible. They navigated past cubicles and came upon a break room with a coffee pot and a small refrigerator and a microwave. Troy left Bonnie standing in the semi-darkness at the break room. Without a sound, he rushed into the large corner office—Gary's office.

Bonnie reached into her pocket, got the last Vicodin, went over to the water dispenser and got a paper cup. With forefinger and thumb, she pulled the blue plastic lever toward her and filled the cup. She swallowed the pill. Then she looked out the front window, looked at the passing headlights and taillights—lights coming and going. There was something wrong out there, she thought, something really wrong. She didn't understand exactly what was going on, but she knew things out there were as crazy as hell. Common decency wasn't common anymore. Then she thought about the little abalone-inlaid pillbox in her underwear drawer where she kept her stash. She frowned. Was the box empty or not? She couldn't remember.

Suddenly Troy was standing in the shadow next to her. Both his fists were closed around the edge of a shellacked diamond-shaped piece of mahogany, upon which was mounted the head of a Thompson Gazelle.

He said, "You didn't touch anything, did you?"

"No, of course not," she answered. And without him seeing, she crumpled the paper cup in her hand and let it fall into the waste can.

THEY MANAGED TO JAM the Tommie's head into the back seat of the Camaro without ripping the upholstery. At first, they tried the trunk, but the lid wouldn't close over the irregular shaped mahogany plaque and backwards curving horns with forward curving tips.

Troy drove to the outskirts of San Jose and veered onto a dirt service road running parallel to some railroad tracks. He drove past a percolation pond until he came upon a vacant field.

He said, "This looks like a good enough spot."

"This is crazy," said Bonnie as she lit a cigarette for herself and her husband. "This whole thing is crazy as hell."

Troy took the cigarette without a word.

Side by side they worked, taking the taxidermy head to a flat spot of earth, heaving it next to a rusted pile of railroad spikes and rotted railroad ties. Then Troy went to the trunk and got a five-gallon can of gasoline. After dousing the Tommie, he took a good look at it—at the black accent stripe dropping from both eyes and the whitish patch on the forehead. Then he tossed his cigarette. Flames whipped the autumn coolness.

Troy used his calloused palm, dragged it across his forehead, wiping away most of the glistening sweat. "I'm not dead yet, baby," he said with a rush of emotion, and he wiped his forehead again. "I still have plenty of fight left in me," he continued as he went back to the trunk for another five-gallon can.

Bonnie stood there, wrapped in cigarette smoke and loneliness. She was tired. She knew her life on Haven Street was over, done with. Strangers in banks and politicians were telling her to start something new. She took a moment to rub her eyes and her mind drifted a bit. She could not help from thinking about the pillbox in her underwear drawer. She frowned. Was it empty? *For the life of me, I can't remember.*

Troy returned to Bonnie's side and unscrewed the cap from the gasoline can. He moved in close to the flames and began shaking the can, immersing the fire with new fuel. Abruptly the tip of gasoline stream ignited, and an orange-red glow followed the stream back into the can. There was a popping sound as the pressurized and heated liquid exploded. Like some kind of firework, liquid fire spewed from the mouth of the can. Troy's reaction was quick. He turned away from the burning Tommie and flung the can away from himself. There was a fiery arc against the night sky then a crash against the roof of Troy's Camaro. Liquid fire spilled down the windshield and onto the hood. Troy hurried to the trunk, fished out an extinguisher. In minutes, the fire was out.

Bonnie moved away from Troy and his cursing, turned her attention to the blaze next to the pile of railroad spikes. Just then, weighted by its backward curling horns, the Tommie's skull tipped to one side. To Bonnie it looked as if it was trying to get out of the mess it had somehow gotten into.

How the hell did you get into this mess? she wondered.

In Need of Repairs

Wayne walked into the family room and went up to his wife, Brenda. She was on the couch, drinking iced coffee and watching television. When Wayne came into the room, she straightened uneasily and began picking at the buttons of her bathrobe.

"I'll be in the garage working on the car," he said.

"Fine."

Wayne hesitated and looked at her. She seemed jittery.

"What's the matter?" he asked. "Seems like there's something the matter."

"Nothing," she said, and she leaned over the coffee table, put her cigarette in the ashtray then eased back into the couch.

"You sure?" he asked.

"Sure I'm sure."

"Well, okay. I'll be in the garage if you need me."

"Sounds good to me," she said picking up the television remote and turning the channel.

Wayne went into the garage and shut the door. For a moment, he stood there, on the doorstep, looking at his '65 Mustang GT Fastback. The car was sanded down to the metal and spotted with body filler and primer spray. It had been difficult getting the car to this point, and he still had much to do.

He pushed the button on the wall, next to the doorjamb. As the garage door rolled open, Wayne ducked under it and looked across the street at Connie. She was on her front lawn, stretched out on a chaise lounge. When she heard the garage door opening she sat up and waved to Wayne. He raised his hand, gave her a smile. She was wearing large frame sunglasses and a leopard print string bikini. Wayne thought she looked like a model in one of those hot rod magazines.

"Working on your car today?" she yelled.

"Putting in a rebuilt carburetor."

"Well, you ought to get outside a bit and enjoy the sunshine," she yelled. Then she adjusted the part of her swimsuit covering her left breast and lay back into the towel.

Wayne walked back into the garage. He took the Johnny Cash cassette tape out of his back pocket and slipped it into the player on the shelf above the washing machine. Then he turned his attention to his car and set to work.

LATER THAT AFTERNOON, when he heard the throaty sound of a Harley Davidson coming down the street, Wayne looked up from the carburetor. He put down the socket wrench, walked outside and stood in the shade of his house at the top of the drive. He watched Jimmy downshift in front of his yard then ride up the driveway. Jimmy cut the idling motor and took off his helmet. He turned and looked at Connie. The sun burned down upon her from a blue, one o'clock sky. She glistened.

Jimmy wiped his forehead. "Son of a bitch," he said, "she's looking fit."

Wayne agreed. "Tell me about it," he said.

Jimmy got a pack of cigarettes from his jacket pocket, put one between his lips, gave one to Wayne.

"Hey," Jimmy said, "you doing any more repairs around her house?"

"Just finished a drywall job."

When Connie first moved into the neighborhood, she had asked for Wayne's help. A wooden plant container in the backyard needed to be moved and she was not strong enough to move it. That had been nearly two years ago. Since then, Wayne had been called upon at different times as she made improvements and repairs to the interior of her house. Recently she had needed some drywalling done to her entryway. When Wayne finished the job, she came up to him. She told him that she had been married to some older guy who owned a couple of used car lots. She married for the wrong reasons; she had told him. Now the only thing she wanted was to be loved. He wanted to tell her that he was sorry for her failed marriage, but suddenly they were talking over each other. Then, just as suddenly, they stopped talking. She looked at him. "I just really appreciate your help in getting this house in shape," she had said. She finished her glass of vodka and orange juice as she led him to the front door.

Jimmy got off his motorcycle and scratched his goatee. "And she still doesn't pay you for any of the work?" he asked.

"Not a dime. I'm a good neighbor."

"Uh-huh. . . and you don't feel used?"

"Really, it's no big deal. She just needs my help is all. We're all in this neighborhood together."

Jimmy looked over to the open car hood and the tools set out on the workbench. "How's the carb coming along?" he asked.

"I'm in the middle of it."

Jimmy pulled on his goatee. "Think you'll have everything ready in time for the show?"

Wayne looked into the garage. The rear seat leaned vertically against the back wall next to the water heater. The windshield lay next to some old barbells. Not just anyone can completely rebuild a car, he thought. Doing a good job on something like this takes time. "Sure," he said. "There's plenty of time before Labor Day weekend."

"I don't know, man, two months'll go by before you know it."

Neither man spoke. Wayne heard some kids down the street throwing a football back and forth. One of the boys kept overthrowing. The other boys were upset about it.

Wayne said, "I'll have it done. Butch said I can use his shop after hours to spray the paint."

"Well, that'll make things easier," Jimmy said. He dropped his cigarette butt on the concrete then went on. "Hey," he said, "I almost forgot. I got this guy and he's got an extra ticket for Sunday's drag race at Infineon. You interested?"

"How much?"

"Ten bucks, he got a deal through his work and bought sixteen tickets. Hell man, it's going to be guy's day out. We're doing a big tailgate ahead of time and. . . I don't know. . . it'll be fun."

"I hear there's going to be over four hundred fifty cars," Wayne said.

"Yeah, it'll be fun."

"I really enjoy the quarter-miler."

"Well, you ought to tag along with us. It'll be fun."

"Tomorrow, huh?"

"Ten bucks. Can't beat it."

Wayne nodded and eased ten dollars from his wallet. Jimmy took the money.

"Good. I'll be fun as hell," Jimmy said as he handed over the ticket.

IT MUST HAVE BEEN an hour after Jimmy hit the road when a furniture delivery truck backed into Wayne's driveway. Wayne stood up and walked over to see what was going on. Two men got out of the cab and went around to the back of the truck. One of them unlocked the tall back door and rolled it open.

"What do you think you're doing?" asked Wayne.

The two men had jumped up into the cargo hold. Now they were coming back carrying a large gold-colored chair, overstuffed and dotted with green and silver circles of various sizes. One of the men bent down and handed Wayne an invoice attached to a clipboard. Wayne looked at it and saw his wife's name and the amount charged to his credit card. Just as he was going to tell them to take the chair back to the store, Brenda came outside. She clutched her bathrobe tight against her body, trying to keep it from opening.

"Don't you dare touch that chair with those greasy hands of yours," she said.

"Alright, Brenda, what the hell is going on here?" Wayne asked.

"Don't get so upset," she said. "It's just a chair I bought."

"Why didn't you tell me?"

"Because."

Wayne put his hands on his hips. "Because why?"

"Because if you knew you would have said no."

"Brenda, I saw the invoice. No one needs a chair that cost this much. The Vice President of the United States doesn't need a chair that costs this much."

She made eye contact with him.

"As ridiculous as it sounds," she said, "this chair is for me not the Vice President of the United States or the President for that matter."

"Okay, that's it," he said. "No way we're keeping that chair."

"That's a matter of opinion," she said.

Wayne turned to the deliverymen. "Take that thing away," he said.

"You're not listening to me," she said. "This chair is staying. It's something for *me*, something *I* want."

Brenda went over to the man holding the clipboard. She used his pen, signed the invoice. As she directed the two deliverymen to follow her into the house, she said, "Honestly, Wayne. Why don't you just get out of their way so they can get on with their job?"

As the men picked up the chair, Wayne looked across the street. Someone had parked a Cadillac in front of Connie's place. Next to the car, Connie stood talking to a woman wearing a fancy pantsuit.

THE FAMILY ROOM WAS silent except for the sound of Brenda moving furniture. Wayne and the two deliverymen watched as she pushed the coffee table closer to the television and scooted the couch and end table down closer to the wall with the window overlooking the front yard and neighborhood. In the silence, Wayne could hear their daughter in her room talking on the telephone. Sissy had just turned twelve and had discovered a certain boy in her sixth-grade class. If she had been born a son, Wayne suddenly thought, he would now be at the age where he could help with the car; help finish things before the Labor Day show.

The men placed the chair in the correct spot and then cleared out.

Wayne watched Brenda sit down in the cushioned seat and cross her legs. His head began to hurt. She had always been a woman of self-control. And now what? Well, he would get things back to normal, he would see to that.

"I thought you were a woman who had her head screwed on right," he said.

"What's that supposed to mean?"

"It means that it's my duty to make sure this household stays afloat, and I don't have a sense of security when money is being spent like this."

She started in on her bathrobe buttons, picking at the pink fabric with her fingernails. "Well, then," she said, "what about you?"

"What about me, what?"

"All that spending on that lousy car."

"I'm not even going to fall for that one," he said.

"What?"

"Getting me off the subject."

"Yeah, well, before the Mustang there was the Corvette and before that the other Mustang."

A thought suddenly came to him and made him angry. Perhaps she did not understand that his goings-on in the garage gave him a strong sense of purpose, made him feel alive. Rebuilding cars was a diversion from work and everything else.

He said, "I know you don't believe me, but spending money on the Mustang is different."

"I don't care a snap what you say. It's not different. Money is money. This whole fixing cars hobby you've planted inside your brain has grown into a huge money sucking habit. And now you're going to this car show and wasting more money."

"Listen, Brenda. You *owe* me an explanation."

"No," she went on. "*You* owe this family a better life than the one you've made. We should have moved by now. Fourteen years of living in this neighborhood—God Almighty! We should be living on the other side of town where Sissy could go to a better school."

"You don't mean that."

"Actually, Wayne, I can't be more serious than I am right now at this moment," she said. She interlocked her fingers, twirled her thumbs.

He stood there for a moment, motionless, wordless, confused. Everything was coming apart, he thought. He turned toward the window and looked outside. Across the street, Connie and the woman were walking across Connie's front lawn toward the house. When they went into the house, Connie shut the door.

Wayne looked down at his wife. He did not have anything more to say, so he said, "Christ, if. . . aw, what's the use." Then he went across the family room and into the garage.

WAYNE FINISHED INSTALLING the carburetor. As he wiped the grease from his hands onto a rag, he took a moment to look over his work. Then he got into the car, turned on the 389 motor, goosed it up. The garage window vibrated. He looked in the rearview. Connie stood at the edge of her driveway while the woman rummaged around for something in the trunk of her Cadillac. When she pulled out a FOR SALE sign and pushed it into the lawn close to the chaise lounge, Wayne turned off the motor.

Wayne shut the garage door and went back into the house. He found Brenda in the family room, sitting in her new chair, watching television.

"Is the chair comfortable?" he asked.

She shushed him. "Shhh," she said, "I'm trying to watch."

He picked up his wife's pack of cigarettes from the coffee table, lit one for himself.

"Maybe we could drive around tomorrow afternoon, take a look at some of those Sunday open houses they always have going on," he said.

"I'll believe it when I see it," she said.

Tomorrow, thought Wayne, he would look in the Sunday paper and make a list of homes. Lists were good and necessary things. He had a list for every phase of rebuilding his car. He put his hand into his front right jean pocket and groaned when he felt the forgotten drag race ticket.

Wayne went into the kitchen and looked out the back window. A section of fence was broken in the rear of the yard. A locomotive and all of its railroad cars was moving south. He watched each car as it passed the downed section of fence.

Then he looked over his shoulder into the family room. His wife sat in her chair. The television was on mute and she was reading some magazine. Beyond her and through the front window he could see Connie's yard. Connie and the chaise lounge were gone. A whirling sprinkler was on. Water sprayed past the FOR SALE sign and out onto the street. Wayne went into the family room. Reluctantly, he sat down on the couch and picked up the television remote.

What a waste of time, he thought.

Plastic Box

Eleanor was reaching for the restaurant door handle when she caught sight of her arthritic knuckles and the array of age spots across the back of her hand. As a young girl, she had spent countless hours playing the piano. She had enjoyed watching the motion of her hands: the curled thrust and pull of her long fingers hammering out a staccato against the weight of the keys. No one had more perfect hands, that's what Robert, her future husband, had told her four decades ago. He had said, your hands are cute and strong looking at the same time, it's a shame you don't get work as a hand model. His own hands were a mess of scars and his fingers littered with broken nails on account of his grind as a heavy equipment mechanic.

Pushing these thoughts aside, she opened the door, letting the smell of freshly cooked tortillas waft past her and into the smoke choked air that stretched across Welderson Valley. She stepped into the air-conditioned environ and went up to the hostess podium. The hostess appeared. Was Eleanor alone? Did she need a table for one? "Oh, no," replied Eleanor, waving to three women at a table in the middle of the room. "I'm meeting some friends."

The hostess grabbed a menu from a plastic holder on the side of the podium then led the way under the vintage looking chandeliers. The restaurant was a cozy arrangement of wooden tables and chairs surrounded by colorful wall decorations: a seven-foot metal sun, brightly painted ceramic plates, murals of reconstructed Mayan temples. As Eleanor approached the table, three women rose from their chairs. They wore overly large shirts covering their aged bodies: bodies that suffered childbirth, sedentary jobs and in one case divorce. They crowded around Eleanor, gave her hugs, squeezed her upper arm, expressed well wishes.

"Come, come sit over here," prompted a women with long wavy burgundy-brown hair, her copper bracelets clinking as she motioned to a chair next to her.

"Thank you," said Eleanor as she eased into the seat. She felt tense, jumpy, and couldn't help from glancing across the restaurant to the large plate glass window. Outside, dark smoke obscured the foothills and heat waves shimmered above the parking lot. According to the morning news, the local air quality was worse than that of Beijing. The thought made her put the back of her hand to her mouth and cough.

"Are you getting somewhat settled?" asked Marcy, the burgundy-brown-haired woman.

Eleanor interlocked her fingers and let her hands rest in her lap. Every time someone asked this of her, she got a pickup-sized lump in her throat. "It's been difficult," she sighed. Clearing her throat she continued, "The fire took everything. Everything except what I was wearing and my plastic box."

Margaret, the divorcée of the group, adjusted her wig and leaned into the table. "Plastic box? What do you mean by plastic box?"

"It's where I keep important papers. You know social security card, birth certificate, tax documents, account numbers, my will. That kind of stuff."

"We keep some of that in our safe deposit box," said Barbara, the woman sitting directly across from Eleanor, "and the rest is scattered around the house."

Margaret returned her attention to Eleanor. "Having everything in one place, ready to go in an emergency is a smart idea."

Through a trembling voice, Eleanor said, "Robert insisted upon it. He got the idea from some financial magazine he flipped through while waiting for his annual teeth cleaning."

Robert had passed nearly two years ago, leaving Eleanor to go it alone. Gone:

the feeling she got during their morning walks and sidewalk conversations;

laughter at dinnertime;

and the setting of unrealistic goals.

When he had been with her, she was a young girl and felt pretty, age spots and loose skin be damned. Gone: that little girl.

"Yes," said Eleanor to her friends around the table, "he insisted upon it. One day Robert got a bug up his butt and put most everything we would need in that plastic box."

A WAITER CAME OVER. Margaritas all around, he said with a smile. The women laughed and looked at each other. Marcy, the burgundy-brown-haired woman, told the waiter it was too early for alcohol.

Eleanor made a show of lifting one hand up above her head and waving it. "Let's see," she said, "I'll have a martini—with three olives."

"Gin or vodka, *ponchita*?" smiled the waiter.

"Gin. . . of course." She turned to her companions. "I don't like those fruity-cocktail things," she said. "Bad for my diabetes, those drinks are." She gave her attention again to the waiter. "And I know what I want to eat."

The waiter put his pen to his pad of order slips.

"I'll have the chicken fajita with a mix of corn and flour tortillas."

The fajita was a large meal, something she and Robert used to split. She was still in the habit of ordering the larger sized menu options. The extra food and lack of morning walks had left her with unwanted weight gain.

As Eleanor's friends gave the waiter their drink and food orders, Eleanor let her mind drift to the violence of the fire three days past. It had started as a summertime grass fire on the side of the highway. But the situation quickly changed. Two weeks of daily temperatures exceeding one hundred degrees had dried out everything. And the unusual forty mile an hour winds whipping through the valley was the match in the powder barrel.

Nearly three thousand structures burned. Fifteen human lives finished. Others missing. Hotels/motels crammed with those fortunate enough to get first dibs. A mass displacement of people filled the county expo parking lot, now crammed with tents and RVs and sleeping bags and dewy-eyed kids running around having fun.

DURING LUNCH, the women broke into separate conversations. Eleanor knew they were nervous, unsure of what to say to their now homeless friend. She also knew they were thinking of their own unburned homes and their good fortune. And so they talked about trivialities and the mundane. Eleanor only half listened:

That's why I eat avocados.

No, a hot dog on a bun is not a sandwich.

You know, my contractor friend told me I should have our heat pump serviced once every year.

Then the conversation became real to her. Burgundy-brown-haired Marcy said:

One theory is that the fire was set by some homeless guy—who was found with $5K of meth. They say he got paid to set the fire.

Eleanor thought that having someone to blame made things easier. And best of all was having someone of bad character to blame, someone other than a careless citizen who fell asleep and dropped a cigarette, or someone who went to the store and left the crockpot plugged in.

Margaret, the divorcée, fiddled with the bangs of her wig before asking: "So, Ellie, how you holding up at your cousin's place?"

After requesting another martini, Eleanor said, "I'm lucky he never got rid of that old camper van."

"But don't it get boiling hot during the afternoon?"

"Oh, yeah it does, that's why I spend the days in his house playing with his grand kids or reading a magazine or watching television. . . sometimes I help with the housework."

Eleanor felt lucky. James, her cousin, knew she was not on good terms with her daughter and two sons, and so agreed to let her stay in his old camper van kept at the back of his property.

"He says I can stay," Eleanor continued, "until I get my feet back on the ground."

Barbara leaned over the tabletop. "Have you been back *there*?" she asked in consolatory tone. "I mean, have you checked out your old home?"

Eleanor nodded while running her tongue under her lips and across her teeth. "Lordy," she blurted, "it looked like a war zone. Like watching some kind of documentary where the anger of war had swept through neighborhoods as far as the eye can see. Everything was completely ravaged except for the chimneys. The chimneys stuck up like dirty statues from the charred rubble. I haven't been able to get a good night's sleep since I went back."

"Oh, you poor dear," said Marcy, and she leaned over and put her fingertips on Eleanor's arm and slowly stroked her skin.

Eleanor slurped on her second martini then said, "Honestly, it's really hard for me to accept all of what's happened. You never think this kind of thing can happen to you."

She used a paper napkin, wiped her mouth. When she returned it to her lap, her mouth was still downturned. The three women waited in silence as Eleanor's memory flashed back and re-rolled the horrible events for the thousandth time. It had been late afternoon. At first, she thought the smoky smell coming into her house was caused by someone in the neighborhood smoking some freshly caught steelhead. Then there had been the pounding at the front door. John, her neighbor, was there. Behind him, flames shot up from the houses across the street. One block over a propane tank exploded. Somewhere a woman was screaming *fire-fire-fire*. The street itself was crammed with traffic, terrified people fleeing in the same direction. It had taken her only a few moments to retrieve the plastic box Robert had put together—he had put the box in the entryway closet, easily accessible during a quick exit. Then John ushered her to the front lawn, where he had parked his car. His wife and two kids were waiting for them. Their eyes were choked with tears and the ash and embers billowing everywhere made them cough and cough. *Thank you, John*, she had said calmly from the back seat.

A busboy came and cleared away the dishes.

Now the women reached under the table and withdrew paper bags containing gift wrapped boxes and envelops. With trembling hands, Eleanor unwrapped the care-packages: calming bath crystals, scented candles, a tin of chocolate confetti cookies, a gift certificate to Costco. And as she read the friendship cards, she was on the verge of tears, but they never came.

"Thank you for all the gifts. Really, they're nice. Really. I appreciate your kindness."

Barbara said, "So are you interested in rejoining the book club?"

Eleanor had not attended the group since Robert's passing. At that time, she had lost interest in reading books. And now the fire. How was she going to pick up all the pieces? Robert would know what to do. Without him around she felt old and out of touch with things.

Abruptly, Eleanor said, "Will you all please excuse me for a moment; I need to visit the restroom."

I SCOOT MY CHAIR AWAY from the table. Sitting in the company of my friends has been rough. Pretending to listen. Vaguely aware of conversation topics. I feel small and insignificant and irritated against their good mood and good fortune. *Get away, get away fast!* My hand shakes as I grab my purse. *Get away.* When I stand and move away from the table the martinis get into my head and fondle my senses. And while teetering down the narrow hallway at the back of the restaurant I recall the time Robert and me went whale watching during our vacation in Astoria, Oregon: the hostile waves, the pitching deck, the seasickness.

My stomach begins to hurt. I hurry into bathroom, slam shut the door. For God's sake, what am I doing here, in this restaurant, pretending my life is not a train wreck? But really, where else would I be? I have nowhere to go. *Ellie has nothing.*

When Robert died, my life veered into unknown territory. Sudden loneliness. Loneliness. Loneliness. But maybe *it* was there all along. Invisible, just out of reach until the right moment, hiding behind my children until they became estranged. Until they became the blamers. Until I became the *blamed.*

Sometimes I feel like slitting my throat with the edge of my AARP card. *Yes, I feel that way!* Robert did it. Not with a plastic card, mind you, but with pills. He was able to endure the hardships and pain of leukemia but was set-off by the ever-present money meter at the hospitals and doctor's office—the great machine sucking up our second mortgage and savings.

Sucking. Sucking. And that's not the half of it. Their ageist attitudes became intolerable to him. *Ageist* is a word Robert introduced to me; even though he had been a lifelong mechanic, he knew things. And so after flailing, flailing, *flailing* away against endless humiliation he gobbled down handfuls of his prescription and the trick was done. His anguish evaporated to nothingness.

I don't blame him for pulling a fast one. None of us are bulletproof.

Oh, Robert.

I put my purse on the countertop surrounding the sink.

I use the toilet.

There is only a few ribbons of paper on the roll. I use it all. When I finish the job, I don't flush right away. Instead, I sit there and think about all those photo albums crammed full of Robert and me. Photo after photo. Photos of birthday celebrations and morning walks and chicken fajitas. Photos no one besides us ever gave a crap about. Photos that burned in the blink of an eye. Gone, just like Robert. *Just like Robert*, I mumble.

Then I think about the pharmacy, the hours standing in line to replenish medication lost in the fire. All the calls to the doctor's office. All the calls to the insurance company. Calls and recalls. Time shriveled away. And still no resolve. No blood pressure pills. No cholesterol pills. Nothing for my IBS. *God, what a cluster fuck!*

Funny, funny. The only prescription medication I have are Robert's old pills. He had ingested only what was necessary. And before the ingestion, he used the emergency plastic box to squirrel away two yellow medicine vials filled with a hodgepodge of pharmaceuticals.

VICODIN.

LORAZEPAM.

TRAZODONE.

Helluva cocktail, Robert. No coming back from that mix. *Why did he gift me these things?* I don't know. It was as if he was being kind, greasing the skids for an especially rainy day.

I flush and pull up my elastic waist pants.

My knees crack as I stand.

My feet feel swollen. Too much salty food. It happens when you're forced to eat restaurant meals and other people's cooking. I miss my crock-pot.

I turn on the sink water. Warm water fills the cup I've made with my palms. I lean forward, massage the water over my face. My pores open to take in the warmth. I have a thing about using paper towels in public restrooms. It's the reason I cart around a square of terry cloth in my purse. As I fumble around for the cloth, I knock my purse to the floor, spilling its contents over the linoleum surface. The yellow medicine vial rolls across the floor, coming to a stop at the base of the toilet. Quickly I use the terry cloth to wipe my face. Then I bend down, shove my belongings into the belly of my purse before going over and retrieving the vial. I straighten up and set the vial on the sink counter. As much as I want to return it to the inside pocket next to my lip balm I don't—I can't. I just stare at it. At this moment, I wish I had flushed its contents when I had first opened the plastic box and discovered Robert's parting gift—his Get Out of Jail Free card. And I am in jail. I can't picture myself ever being happy again. I can't picture myself pulling the fragmented pieces of my life together into a fresh start. The destruction of my home and possessions and *history* with Robert intensifies feelings that have suffocated me since finding his body in the garden shed in the back of our lot. Any chance of recalibrating to normalcy has been purged by that fucking fire. Burned. Up in smoke, as they say. Yes, I wish I had flushed those pills. But I didn't.

No more thinking. I'm tired of thinking. Exhausted.

I twist off the lid from the vial and spill half of its contents onto the countertop. Nine white tablets. More than enough. I raise my sight to the mirror. Stare at myself. It seems that the structure of my face has changed. My eye sockets look wider than when I was a young woman. And my jawline looks somewhat different. And over this foundation stretches droopy, flabby, blotchy skin. *Is this me?* How? When did all this happen? How did I get so old? The face looking back at me is not Robert's little girl. My feelings are impossible for me to control. With the edge of my left palm, I brush the pills from the counter and into the palm of my right hand.

I'm not sure how long I stare at that white pile between the base of my thumb and little finger. I'm still staring when the bathroom door opens and Marcy enters. Suddenly I'm conscious of her presence. I curse under my breath, turn to face her. Right away she knows the shape of things. I thought she'd be angry and start bitching at me, but she just stands there, silent. Her feelings don't show on her face, there is no look of surprise, just a litter of broken capillaries sitting atop a turkey neck.

She steps in closer. Our toes are almost touching.

"Are those Robert's pills?" she asks.

"They were. Now they're mine," I say.

"Look," she says, "This horrible fire-thing stinks, but as bad as it seems it will pass. You can rebuild."

I close my fingers around the pills. Clinch my fist. "It's not about the fire, Marcy. It's about Robert."

"Oh, you poor dear."

"I mean, yes my house is now a trash hole, but it's Robert that's plaguing me. And I've had enough. . . I just want to fade away—fast forward to the end of things."

Marcy nonchalantly brushes a length of hair from her face. "Oh, Ellie," she continues, "You did nothing wrong. It was out of your control. I hope you realize this."

"Hope? There's no kind of hope that can lift this sorrow."

I can feel the roundness of the pills against the skin of my palm. They don't feel as welcome as they did only a few minutes ago.

Marcy senses my hesitation. "Have you tried calling some sort of hotline?"

"Yes. Many times."

"Did it help?"

"Yes, sometimes."

"Why didn't you come to me, or one of the girls? We're here for you. You know this don't you?"

"I don't want to be a burden to anyone."

"Oh, Ellie, You are family to us."

Marcy takes my fist into her right hand while her left hand peels back my fingers. She takes the pills and returns them to the vial, Then she buries the vial deep into her purse—the tomb of my indiscretion. She says, "Do you have any more in the camper van at your cousin's place?"

I take the terry cloth from my purse and wipe my eyes. "No, no," I say. "This is it. This is all of them."

Marcy knows I'm lying, but she doesn't call me on it. "I think," she says, "it's time for you to rejoin our book club. We miss you something awful. It's just not the same without you. Will you come back?"

Good Lord, Ellie, what are you waiting for? "I miss you guys," I whisper, "I've wanted to return, but the circumstances never seemed to be right."

"Well, now is the time." She fuses with the strap of her purse and says, "Come on, our friends are out there waiting for you to rejoin them. Shall we. . ."

Her comfort is like windshield wipers against my sadness. Again, I work the dampened terry cloth over my eyes. "I look terrible."

She hugs me, talks into my ear. "You look fucking great," she says. "Like some kind of princess."

MARCY GAVE ELEANOR'S UPPER ARM a friendly squeeze as they moved from the bathroom to the hallway. The disorder that had jammed Eleanor's head a moment past began to clear, and she became aware of the festive Mexican music coming from speakers tucked away in the ceiling—an accordion soloing over a foundation laid down by guitar, guitarrón, vihuela and violin. In time with the music, Eleanor tapped her forefinger against the side of her thigh as she entered the dining area. My piano-fingers, she thought. And as they approached the table, Eleanor whispered to her friend. *Lips sealed, yes?* Marcy leaned into Eleanor. *Our little secret*, she whispered back.

With smiles, Margret and Barbara welcomed their return.

Eleanor struggled to control her emotions as she seated herself. In front of her remained two fingers of her second martini. She polished it off with a quick movement before settling back in her chair.

"What were you two whispering about?" asked Margaret.

"Yes," said Barbara, "We saw you whispering . . ."

Marcy lifted her arms above her head and wobbled her hands "Uh-hummm. . ." she said, "we have a bit of good news to share. Ellie will be rejoining our book club. Isn't that right, Ellie?"

Eleanor confirmed the announcement. "I don't know what took me so long to get back in the saddle," she said.

The women clapped and voiced their happiness.

Then Barbara gave Eleanor a very serious look. "Well," she said, "it seems this long-awaited occasion deserves something special. Margaret. . ."

Margaret leaned over and fished a nicely gift-wrapped box from under the table. "Here," she said. "We got this for you as a parting gift. But it also makes a great gift for good news."

Wrapped in pink paper, the present was cereal box in size and shape. Some sort of book, thought Eleanor. Maybe one of those self-help things. She wiped her knife on the napkin resting on her lap and went to work; hand trembling as she slit the blocks of tape covering the seams of paper. Abruptly she inhaled with surprise as the paper fell away and the ornate photo album cover came into view.

Nobody talked as she opened to a random page. What does anyone say when looking at snapshots of deceased loved ones? Eleanor was silent as her attention focused on Robert doing a cannon ball in the shallow end of the Y.M.C.A. pool. He hung above the water, eyes closed, cheeks puffed, lungs air-filled. It had been Marcy's sixty-fifth that day, she recalled. A crew of friends had spent the afternoon watching college football at Buffalo Wild Wings, and then pool partied at the Y. So there was Robert, the life of the party, enjoying his life. Her mind let her hear the shouts of encouragement, the laughing. As her eyes roved around the snapshot, she made up her mind. *I am no longer the blamed. To hell with what her kids believed.*

Eleanor closed the book. She rested her piano-fingers on the back of Marcy's hand. "Thank you, Hon," she said. Then she scanned the faces around the table. "I couldn't have better friends," she said. "Thank you for preserving my memories."

Her friends were now wadding up their paper napkins and piling them on top of their dirty plates. Each acknowledged Eleanor's comment with a smile or some small pleasantry. Barbara had already picked up the tab, paid for everyone's meal. They pushed back their chairs and gathered up their purses.

Marcy stood up, looked down at Eleanor. "Ready, to hit the road, Ellie?"

But Eleanor was in no hurry to return to the camper van at the rear of the backyard. The small space would be furnace hot by now. And sitting in the house listening to her cousin's grandkids go on about making blanket forts in the living room was not particularly appealing at the moment.

Eleanor looked up at Marcy. "I'm not ready to leave just yet. I'm enjoying the air conditioner in here," she said running the palm of her hand over the photo album cover. "And I think," she continued, "I'm going to stay a bit longer and take my time going through these memories."

"You want some company?"

"No, thank you. This is a private thing. I just want to be alone with my feelings."

"Well, I'll see you at the next book club gathering, right?"

"Yes. Count on it," she said.

Each of Eleanor's friends gave her a hug or a cheek-kiss then left.

Eleanor motioned to the waiter across the room. He saw her waving hand and hurried over.

"Yes, *ponchita*? Is there anything else I can get you?" he asked.

"I'll have a martini—with three olives."

"Very good. One gin martini coming up," he said.

As he moved away from the table, Eleanor raised her hand again and waved. "Excuse me," she said.

The waiter turned and looked at her.

"Can you please make it an iced tea instead?" she said.

Polka Dots

SATURDAY.
Mid-afternoon.

Buell, standing in the middle of the kitchen, opened his beer, guzzled it down. Every night that week he had stayed late at the cement plant, drinking and playing poker with some of the other workers. Now his head hurt and he felt dehydrated and he imagined his brain as a tightly shriveled walnut-sized thing.

A boy came into the kitchen. He brought with him a large empty cardboard box with wheels drawn on each side.

"Hey daddy, wanna see the button that makes the horn honk?"

Buell drank his beer and watched the boy get into the box.

"It's the H-Button," said the boy. "You push it and the sound goes Honk. H O N K!"

Buell's face tightened. "Okay, that's enough of that, Adam. Daddy's trying to think, so I want you to go in the other room and play."

"But daddy, I want to show you. Look, daddy."

Buell looked at his reflected face in the kitchen window, watched himself light a cigarette. He said, "Come on, Adam, go play in the TV room."

The boy looked up at Buell. "If I put the flaps out it's a flying fish," he said.

Buell crushed the cigarette in the sink then went down the hallway and talked to Vicky in the bathroom. She had to push aside a corner of the shower curtain and crane her neck to understand his words. Water dripped onto the linoleum, pooled around the base of the toilet.

"What?" she said with a small amount of irritation in her voice.

Buell stood at the edge of the bathroom, where carpet met linoleum. "I said. . . I'm going over to the *One Stop* to get a pack of smokes."

"Well okay," she said, blinking soap from her eyes, "but come straight home. The head of ICU has been getting on my case about being late these days." She closed the curtain then pushed it aside again. "While you're at it," she said, "will you pick up some Pop-Tarts? We're all out of Pop-Tarts. Frosted Cherry flavored, okay?"

"Sure," he said. "Cherry flavored."

Vicky's mother spoke up from the spare room. "*Frosted* Cherry!" she hollered. "Frosted Cherry Pop-Tarts, you good-for-nothing jackass. And don't come back with no liquor. You know how the Lord feels about liquor."

Buell looked into the spare room. His mother-in-law was in her robe, reclining on the foldout bed, looking for discounts on shoes in the Pennysaver.

"Sweet Jaaaysus. . . if I can just loosen your hold on Vicky and get you out of the house and back with your old man maybe things around here would get back to normal," he said.

"Just get them Frosted Cherry ones," she said without looking up from the newspaper.

Buell had nothing more to say so he went to the closet next to the front door, reached behind the broom and grabbed the travel bag he'd packed one night before going to bed.

BUELL HURRIED DOWN his apartment steps to the sidewalk. Exhaust fumes and honking horns jammed the city air. He walked two blocks to a liquor store. Next to the cash register, a radio played Mariachi music. A Latina emerged from a back room. She pulled back her hair and secured it with a rubber band from around her wrist.

"The usual?" she said.

"Yep."

"Anything else?"

"Nope, just a pint of Beam and a pack of Marlboros."

She stretched on tiptoes, got the pint from a shelf behind the counter and put it in a paper sack. He gave her exact change.

Outside, he worked his lighter against a cigarette. Then he went across a vacant lot, peeled back a small section of chain link fence, slipped through, went across a street to the Seasons Motel and made his way toward room #107. When his knocking went unanswered, he tried the doorknob and found it unlocked.

THE ROOM WAS DARK behind closed drapes and reeked of stale beer. On the queen mattress, a man lay on his stomach, head turned to the right, mouth open, black hair greasy and disheveled.

From the bathroom came a woman, naked, no tan-lines, navel glinting with a rhinestone stud. A green butterfly tattoo with baby's feet instead of wings engulfed the fullness of her left breast. When she saw Buell, she went over to the small dresser next to the television. She sat down and let her legs dangle against the dresser drawers.

"Hi," she said in a tired and hoarse voice, "I'm Rachel."

"I'm Buell," he said. He pointed to the bed. "That there's Uncle Jeff. He raised me after my daddy died." Without air conditioning, the room was a furnace. Buell's armpits became wet and began to stink, but he didn't notice. He went on talking, telling Rachel about Vicky and about cutting out on her. "Ran like a rabbit with his balls on fire," he said as he went over to his suitcase and got the sack. "You known Uncle Jeff for very long?" he asked after taking a pull of Beam.

"Met him last night at the *Last Call*," she said. "He needed a partner for doubles pool and I'm a pretty good shooter."

"Huh," said Buell, looking at the stained carpet and listening to the sound of traffic on the boulevard. Already he missed Vicky, but he didn't miss her nagging. He turned from Rachel and went outside, cleared his nostrils onto the concrete walkway and sat down in a plastic chair, tipping it back against the motel wall. He was bone-weary and disgusted with himself for being too tired to go back into the room for the forgotten whisky.

RACHEL WALKED UP TO BUELL. She wore round sunglasses, cut-off jeans and a t-shirt and carried two cans of Miller. Buell took the beer and gave up the chair. She reclined, stretching out her legs, crossing them at the ankles.

"You know," she said, "Sometimes you got to leave things behind so you could move forward—one step back, two steps forward. We all do it."

Buell grunted. "My old lady don't think so," he said. "She's got this idea in her head that things work themselves out given enough time." He lit a cigarette and continued. "Then there's the Scriptures. As if working that cussed rock grinding press all day long ain't enough, she's got to go and bible-thump me whenever she's got the chance."

"Jesus."

"You said it. I feel like a rubber band stretched to the point where I can't stretch no more without snapping."

Rachel leaned forward and her eyes brightened. "Hey," she whispered.

"What?"

"The sun, look how insanely beautiful it is—the different tints of colors, the long shadows it's making on the earth."

The sun seemed to hover above the distant foothills rimming the Santa Clara Valley. Then it descended.

She said, "Sometimes I write poetry about things like sunsets and birds in flight and grassy meadows and bright pink fuchsias. I love fuchsias. Don't you? Don't you just love fuchsias?"

Buell turned his attention to her profile, noticed her cute dimple. He looked down at her feet, at the thin blond hair curling over her toe knuckles. He wanted to see her naked again, wanted to touch her face with his fingertips, wanted her to distract him from life. His cigarette bounced between his lips as he talked. He said, "Not sure what fuchsias are, Rachel. But I'll bet they're something to see."

BUELL AND RACHEL stayed outside, drinking and laughing and smoking cigarettes. After a while, headlights moved onto Buell's chest as a dented car rolled into a parking spot in front of him. Through the windshield, he saw Vicky's face. Vicky turned off the headlights and got out of the car. She walked to the front bumper and stood there rubbing her fingers over the scarification between shoulder and elbow where as a teenager she had used an open paperclip to carve a dragonfly into her skin. Buell thought she looked attractive in her white and black sleeveless polka dot sundress. He had given it to her on their first Christmas together. They had spent that Christmas Eve in her apartment, on the couch, eating in front of the television. "That's a helluva thing to do," he had said after she squeezed lemon juice over her corndog. She laughed and laughed and squeezed more juice. Then he leaned into her and put his lips against her hair. "You're angel-pretty," he had said. The words filled her youthful heart, delighted her, made her roll onto her back, made her slide the polka dot dress to her hips.

Vicky became tearful. "I said the sinner's prayer for you today," she said.

Buell rolled his eyes. It was almost funny how she always showed up before he fully embraced freedom. "No one is asking you say no prayers for me, Vicky," he said roughly. "I don't want no prayers. I just want to be left alone."

"Benjamin Buell Davis stop this foolishness once and for all and come home where you belong," she said. "You need to get onto the path of salvation."

Buell looked at Rachel. "See what I mean? You see? Just like that she shows up and busts my balls, tries to run my life."

Rachel flicked ash from her cigarette onto the concrete and spoke up, told Vicky to live and let live.

Buell shifted his weight from one foot to the other. "I'm staying," he said. "I'm staying here and you should get to work before that ICU manager of yours fires your skinny ass."

"Hon," she said, "look around. There's nothing for you here, and that's God's own truth."

Across the street, a man moved back and forth in the twilight, running a metal detector over the strip of weeds at the edge of the road, listening for beeps through his headphones.

Buell shook his head. "Nope, there's no sense in talking about it no more," he said. "So you just get on home without me."

Vicky straightened. "Please don't do this in front of the children!" she shouted.

Buell and Rachel suddenly noticed the two snotty nosed boys and baby girl in the rear seat. Rachel took a good look then stood up and dropped her cigarette into her beer can. As she made her way back to the motel room, she avoided Vicky's eyes.

Vicky wiped her eyes. "Stop being hurtful and come home before it's too late," she said. "Please let Jesus help you."

"You mean like He helped you?"

"*He'll* only open the door if you knock."

Buell looked at his kids. Adam's wailing unraveled him.

She beckoned him. "Just come home," she repeated. "I know we can get through this rough patch."

She returned to the driver's seat, reached over and unlocked the passenger door. Then she started the motor and sat, hands on the steering wheel, waiting. Buell cussed and bounced his beer can off the windshield. Beyond the parking lot, the man with the metal detector reached down and picked up something from the weeds. Buell watched the man gingerly work a brush over the wallet-sized object, and it seemed to him that everyone he knew was lonelier than not. Somehow, they had been dispossessed of childhood thoughts and dreams.

Buell got into the passenger seat and shut the door. In the rear seat, the two boys sniffled and made whining sounds and the baby girl's fat face was wet with tears. Buell thought he was living through the worse day of his life. He needed a cigarette and suddenly noticed he had left his on the plastic chair against the motel wall. He opened the glove to see if Vicky had a pack stashed away. When the door swung open, a dog-eared bible choked with bookmarks fell onto his lap. Buell recognized it as the bible Vicky had snatched from their motel room in Idaho the time they had picked up her mother and brought her back to California. The theft was Vicky's turning point, her path to sobriety, to wellbeing.

Vicky leaned over and put her hand on the scuffed book cover. "I got this hopeful feeling," she said moving her hand from the book cover to Buell's shoulder and letting her fingers play with the edge of his collar, "I just know you're going to surprise yourself."

Buell returned the book to the compartment and shut the door.

"I'm sorry for doing this, again," he said.

She smiled. "I know you are, baby."

"You'll see. This time I mean it. I can do better. You can trust me. No more drinking sprees, I promise. I'll stop drinking for good and I'll treat you better."

"I know you will, baby," she said. "I have faith in you."

Buell cleared his throat. "Can you ever forgive me? I mean, do you have it in you to forget all this?"

"I don't blame you for none of this, so there's nothing to forgive," she said. And then she added, "You're still my baby, still my dream-boy."

Buell leaned back in the passenger seat, stared at his folded hands resting in his lap.

"I like your dress," he whispered.

"I know you do," she said.

Small Town Blues

As Jennings steered his pickup from North Oak Street into a small parking lot in need of resurfacing, he worked his jaw muscles and chewed hard against the toothpick in the corner of his mouth. He drove across the lot and found a spot under a thirty-foot Robin made of re-bar, chicken wire and fiberglass. When he turned off the motor, the muffler shook and dark smoke came up from the exhaust pipe. Jennings stepped out from the cab and spat his toothpick onto the ground. He was a lanky man and wore a loose-fitting black front-button shirt and a pair of abused-looking steel toe work boots. He grabbed a shopping cart and slowly pushed it past the plate glass doors and into the store.

Inside, he bypassed the hunting and fishing aisles and turned into the garden aisle. After piling three rolls of 3-inch x 25-foot lengths of flexible drainage hose into his cart, he moved to the far side of the Giant Robin and got a package of duct tape. All of this labor and money just to kill his neighbor's rooster, he thought. The entire affair was depressing. He'd always had a soft temper, slow to anger, but that white trash Wyman had left him no choice. At first, Jennings believed he could diplomatically solve the problem. Several times he and his girlfriend, Charlene, had gone next door to Wyman's place, told him that the rooster was disturbing them at god-awful hours. "You see, you've put the rooster along the property line, forty-five feet from our bedroom window," explained Jennings. "Maybe if you moved him to the backside of your half-acre it would help things." When Wyman ignored the request, Jennings gave the county code enforcement officer a call. He discovered the damndest thing. Not a single noise ordinance stretched beyond the city limits into the country. A call to the local sheriff confirmed his findings. The sheriff said, "Sounds like it's time to go rooster hunting." "Really?" asked Jennings. After a short silence the sheriff said, "No, not really." He told Jennings to keep to his own business and not to harass his neighbor and went on to say, "Are you listening to me?" "Yes, I hear you," said Jennings.

As Jennings put the items onto the checkout conveyor belt, his mouth became dry. There's no getting away from what needs to be done, he told himself.

The cashier coughed to get his attention. Then she said, "That'll be $75.19."

Jennings blinked a few times. "Hang on there a sec.," he said, and he leaned over the conveyor. His hand quivered as he pulled the latest *Field & Stream* from the magazine rack. "I guess you could add this onto the total."

"Sure thing," she said, and she scanned the bar code on the front cover.

JENNINGS LEFT THE BIG ROBIN and headed home. He drove past the newly painted Baptist church at the edge of town and made his way along roads lined with barbed wire fences. Beyond the fences grew tall yellow grass and oaks, thick with leaves flittering in the spring breeze. As he drove, Jennings chewed on a toothpick. Hell, he told himself, that no good piece of white trash and his damn rooster deserve what's coming to them. He recalled a time when Wyman was talking to his mother who lived in a trailer between the edge of the street and the chicken coop. Jennings remembered leaning over the hedge running along the property line and speaking his mind.

"Sometimes I got to work swing shift and it's hard to get some shut-eye when your rooster's going at it all morning long." Jennings had just started a new job—draining and cleaning residential and commercial septic pumps—every fourth day from 4pm to 8am he was on-call for troubleshooting. Wyman had looked over his shoulder, grinned at Jennings, showed his false teeth. "Listen," he said, "if you don't want to hear no rooster then you go on and shut your window." His belly moved with laughter. Jennings felt like cracking Wyman's head with a baseball bat, but he remembered that the sheriff had advised him against making trouble.

Jennings drove over the small wooden bridge spanning the roadside irrigation ditch. Once on his street he abruptly slammed on his breaks as Grandma Wyman's dog trotted out in front of his pickup and stood there barking at his left tire. Twenty-five feet away, Grandma Wyman sat on her trailer step, watching her barking dog and saying nothing about it. Jennings slowly moved around the dog and went down his gravel driveway. Charlene was on the front porch, smoking a cigarette, waiting for him. Her blond hair hung in a thick ponytail against her back, and she wore cut-off jeans and red synthetic leather boots. A black spaghetti strap half shirt showed off her belly, tan and pregnant swollen. He had to hand it to her; she was now down to two smokes a day and making an effort to be healthy for the baby.

Jennings parked in the garage next to his bass boat. He got out and hurried to his driveway, where he reached down and grabbed a handful of gravel. He threw the gravel at the barking dog.

"Stay off my property you damn white trash mutt," he yelled.

Charlene talked to him from the porch. She rubbed one hand over her belly and told him about the rooster. "Son of a bitch rooster's been going all day long," she said.

Suddenly the rooster began to crow. *Cockadoodledoo! Cockadoodledoo!*

She continued, "Baby, you got to make Wyman get rid of that thing before I lose my mind!"

"Just simmer down," he said. "Things are under control."

"How can things be under control when that damn rooster is alive and crowing?"

He had met Charlene during the neighborhood hockey season, during one of his Wednesday night games. She was new behind the rink grill and they hit it off right away when Jennings went for an after game burger. At that time, she was going through a divorce and still a little thick in the middle from having her first kid, the one now living with her mother. But she was a looker all the same, with her blond hair and eyes pale blue. When she got pregnant neither of them had any doubts about her move into his place, it was only when their neighbor bought a rooster that problems kicked in. "Why'd you get that rooster, anyway?" Jennings asked Wyman at the start of it all. "I like fertilized eggs," he had said. "Jesus, you mean to eat? You mean to tell me that you eat sperm eggs?" For a good half year, during morning, noon and early evening there had been no quietude. *Cockadoodledoo, cockadoodledoo!* The rooster crowed continuously throughout the day. Finally, things came to a head. The rooster was crowing away one morning when Charlene turned on the lamp alongside of the bed and pushed the quilt comforter from her body. It was very dark outside. Convince me that you're my man; she had told Jennings in a raised voice. Convince me! In that instant, he knew he needed to solve the problem once and for all, nip it in the bud. But how to handle the matter? The solution came to him on a Sunday afternoon while watching a TV documentary about Death Row within San Quentin.

On the porch, Charlene stomped her booted foot hard against the oak planks. "Go on and tell me," she yelled. "How are things under control? Nothing has changed! Nothing is ever going to change!"

"Look, everything changes sometime," he said in a lowered voice and he crossed the driveway and went behind her and put his arms around her swollen waist. Earlier he'd decided not to explain his idea to gas the rooster with carbon monoxide. He didn't want to worry her, didn't want to disturb the baby. He wanted a smooth birth without unnecessary worrying.

THEY STOOD TALKING IN THE KITCHEN as Charlene fixed white bread and bacon sandwiches. Jennings waved his beer can around in front of him as he talked. Charlene had just suggested moving to the coast, somewhere around Eureka, to a nice apartment overlooking the Pacific. If they moved to the coast, there would be no rooster problem.

"My work is here," he said pointing his beer can toward Charlene, "not on the coast."

"Well you're a jack of all trades; can't you just get a different job?"

"Jesus Char," he said, "how can you say that when work is finally going well. Besides, we both know the house would be on the market for a good year before it sold." Jennings knew this to be true. Somehow, he'd gotten himself into a situation where he couldn't afford to move.

Charlene finished coating two slices of bread with mayonnaise, and then sandwiched the bacon. "Here," she said then she leaned back against the counter and used her hands to cup her belly. "When's the last time you've seen yourself in the mirror, huh?" she asked. "Bags and dark circles under your eyes. You're not even thirty-five but you've got the bags of a sixty-year-old. You never had bags when I first met you."

"It's on account of the new job. . ." Jennings began.

Charlene interrupted. "What's the matter with you, huh? It's that rooster. Being constantly bombarded by that white trash rooster isn't healthy; it isn't healthy for the three of us."

Outside, along the property line, forty-five feet from their bedroom window the rooster crowed and crowed and crowed. *Cockadoodledoo!*

Charlene quietly finished her sandwich then went to the living room with her beadwork kit and turned on the radio. Jennings joined her, sitting himself down on a sofa pushed against the wall and beneath a window overlooking the backyard and the bordering apple orchard and the distant mountains, still capped with spring snow. He put a toothpick between his teeth and opened *Field & Stream*. It was a warm evening and the window was open to let in the slight breeze coming down from the north. When the rooster began to crow Jennings got up and shut the window. Still the sound came through the glass. *Cockadoodledoo!*

"Good Christ," mumbled Jennings as he picked up his magazine and leaned back into the cowhide sofa cushions.

THE SUN WENT DOWN and crickets came out, filling the night with soft chirping. Charlene held up a coin purse and admired her beaded handiwork, a repeating pattern of red and turquoise diamonds.

"What do you think?" she asked Jennings.

"Looks Native American," he said.

"Supposed to look that way."

"What is it?"

"It's a coin purse I'm going to use for Baby's teeth."

Charlene stared at the beaded design and Jennings had the idea she was lost in thought about how the court had decided in favor of her mother for guardianship of her daughter. Someday, he thought, he would help her win back custody, but he needed to move up in his job before that happened. He needed to get off the shoestring from which he was dangling.

Charlene closed her beadwork kit and told Jennings she was tired, that it was past her bedtime and that he should go to bed too. She said, "You need your sleep, baby, so don't stay up too late."

Jennings told her that he was going to the garage for a while. "I want to tie a few fishing flies," he said. "The trout are biting on cicada patterned flies and I don't have any of those."

In the garage, he flipped on the overhead fluorescents, opened all four windows and got a beer from the fridge next to the sink. He was thirsty and the beer tasted good, and it put something in his blood that made him get down to nitty-gritty. He retrieved the three rolls of hose from his pickup, tore away the plastic packaging and connected the lengths with duct tape, creating a flexible pipeline seventy-five feet long. Then he duct taped the hose over the tailpipe of his truck. That ought to keep the carbon monoxide from seeping into the garage, he thought.

After taking a few swallows of beer, he turned off the overhead fluorescents, opened the side door, picked up the hose and uncoiled it from the garage to the hedge at the property line, head lowered and eyes sharp as he walked the distance. The crickets became silent and to Jennings the night suddenly seemed different, a place to be avoided. He was normally in bed sleeping at this hour but now he was outside, squatting, knees nearly touching chin, pushing a drainage hose through leaves and branches. When the end of the hose butted against the wire rooster pen, he drew a deep breath and held it for a moment, listening. In the nearby trailer, Grandma Wyman's dog began to bark. This wasn't unusual. The dog barked every night. Ten yards away the chickens became restless in their coop and began to cluck. He knew he was doing a bad thing, and so had to remind himself of his futile conversations with the county office and the sheriff. What the hell was wrong with these people? How could they ignore something so obviously wrong?

Jennings went back to the garage. Inside it was dark. He felt his way around stacks of Charlene's unpacked boxes before finding his truck. Quickly but carefully, he checked the hose-tail pipe connection, making sure he hadn't inadvertently jarred things loose. Then he got into the cab and started up the motor. To hell with Wyman, he thought, and he went over to the workbench and got his can of beer. But the can was empty, so he got another from the fridge and went outside to the wooden bench next to a pit where they had once buried a pig and cooked him Hawaiian-style. He sat in the darkness, listening. The crickets had begun to chirp again, though they had moved further down the hedge where the air was much fresher. Beyond the crickets, a small pack of coyotes yelped as they made their way through the apple orchard to the creek where they hunted muskrat and rabbits. Jennings leaned back on the bench, drinking his beer, feeling happy that the sound of his truck motor could not be heard.

After a good hour, Jennings went to his garage. Right away, his eyes became sore and watery and it was difficult for him to hold back a fit of coughing. He took a deep breath and hurriedly turned off the truck motor. Then he opened the garage door and let in the warm breeze. The air around him became clean enough to go to the exhaust pipe where he detached the hose. Back at the hedge, he withdrew the hose from Wyman's side yard and tried to see the rooster, but it was too dark. When he rattled the bush a little, there were no sounds of movement. He returned to the garage and put the hose in the attic, closed the garage door, shut the windows and entered his house.

Charlene was sleeping but stirred a little when he kissed her cheek. It was late and Jennings should have been tired, but exhilaration made him wide-awake. He went to the kitchen and got himself a bowl of *Captain Crunch*. He took it to the TV room where he plopped down on the sofa and thought about the baby. The doctor had told them that the baby would be boy. Jennings smiled, a boy, he thought. For a moment he felt as fine as cream gravy then he went back to his cereal.

THE NEXT MORNING Jennings awoke, sat upright and looked at the bedside clock—6:35. He'd slept nearly two and a half hours longer than he would have on any given day. He felt rested, the most rested he'd felt in nearly six months. Charlene was right; he didn't know how much the rooster had affected his life. Now the world, which had seemed so very far away, came back to him and he was glad he did what he did and he didn't care if that lousy white trash Wyman got another rooster so long as there was a few days of silence.

He got dressed for work and found Charlene in the kitchen, bending over the stove, making eggs-in-a-hole, working the spatula under a corner of the bread and peeking at its underside. She wore her favorite yellow bathrobe, now stretched out of shape around her belly.

"Must be something wrong with that white trash rooster," she said.

Jennings smiled. "I'm going out to get the paper."

Outside he walked the length of his gravel driveway to the edge of his property and the post mounted mailbox. Across the street, several neighbors had gathered around Roy Turner in his driveway. Turner waved to Jennings. "Old lady Wyman," he shouted with an uneasy voice, "she died last night!"

Jennings looked toward Grandma Wyman's trailer. The door was open and Wyman stood on the wooden steps leading to the entry. He had formed a cradle with his arms and draped over his shirtsleeves lay Grandma Wyman's mutt, tongue hanging out, swollen and black. As Wyman talked to the two police officers his face remained as emotionless as cut stone.

Jennings went back into his house and rushed into the bathroom. He was splashing water from the sink tap onto his face when the doorbell rang. Charlene came into the bathroom and told Jennings that the police were at the door. "They want to have a word with you," she said.

Jennings looked at his hands hanging limp at his sides. He knew he was on shaky ground. He had suffocated his dream with Charlene and God wasn't going to let him get away with it. For a long moment he wondered if she would move to the coast without him. Then he looked up at the ceiling and saw the blue painter's tape stuck over the vent fan, put there to mask the rooster's crowing, which had found its way down the pipe sticking out from the rooftop. Jennings balanced himself as he stepped onto the toilet seat. He reached one hand up toward the ceiling and peeled the tape away from the fan.

"There," he said to Charlene. "Finally, we can use the ventilation fan whenever the shower is going." Still standing on the toilet seat, he took a small, plastic container from his shirt pocket and tapped out a toothpick. As he put the toothpick between his teeth, he looked down at his girlfriend and he knew the memory of seeing her swollen belly from that angle would forever be with him.

Adoration for Jill

THE TRAFFIC LIGHT CLICKS to yellow and Wade Nickles guns his '66 El Camino. In the intersection the cigarette lighter pops. He takes it, touches it to the Camel Light dangling from his lips. He goes down Blossom Hill, past Taco Bell and Home Depot, and turns right onto Old Monterey Highway. Then he makes a quick left into the *Rio Guadalupe Mobile Home Park*. He pulls up in front of the double-wide Jill is renting, gets out and takes a final inhale of his cigarette before dropping it to the ground.

The late afternoon sunshine stretches over the San Jose metropolitan area and pushes hard against things, making shadows short and stubby. Wade takes off his Raider's cap and hangs it on the gun rack in the rear window. The sun pushes through his thinning hair and he thinks about his maternal grandfather's baldness. Wade doesn't want to become bald and thinking about it drives him crazy, makes him sometimes fish for compliments. Suddenly some Latin pop music blares from a mobile across the street and snaps him back to the moment.

Wade steps over a small pink bike and moves up the wheelchair ramp the previous owner had built after her auto accident—before she moved into one of those assisted living arrangements, before Jill moved in last spring. He moves up the ramp to the rectangular cutting of plastic grass and stops. The television is going loud. He rings the bell. Doubts about their dating bloat within him. After four dates, he believes Jill wants to call it quits. He doesn't have any hard evidence to support this belief. Just a feeling is all. And he's afraid to confess his suspicions outright, afraid she would marginalize his affection toward her. With outstretched arm he leans against the aluminum siding. But the metal is hot, so he uprights himself.

JILL OPENS THE DOOR and stands there pushing mousy bangs from her face with one hand and holding an Oreo cookie with the other. She's all done up (purple mid-riff tank, jeans tight against willowy legs and cuffed at the ankles, cheetah-patterned pumps) for a dinner at Earl's Spit Broil and pool at DeLux Billiards. Between her shirt and jeans, faint stretch marks on exposed skin run north and south like train rails.

Wade says, Hey, Jill, you're looking damn hot tonight.

Listen, says Jill popping the Oreo into her mouth, I got some bad news.

She tells him the neighbor lady, Alicia Marie Sanchez, hasn't showed up. Alicia Marie is supposed to babysit. But she's late, so now they have to wait. Wade looks past Jill, into the small area designated as the living room. Jill's daughter, Temmy, is there in her pajamas, fixed in front of the television.

Wade stretches his neck into the double wide. Whatcha watching, Temmy? he asks.

Temmy doesn't hear the question, or maybe she simply ignores him. He doesn't know.

Jill looks over her shoulder and says, Buttercup, you ought to answer when you're being talked to. Then she says to Wade, I'll tell you what, Temmy's been streaming Princess Barbara movies all afternoon.

Temmy wipes her snot-nosed and speaks up. She says, Look at the chill car Barbara's boyfriend drives. All of Barbara's boyfriends drive chill cars.

Wade steps through the doorway and Temmy turns up the volume.

Might as well get comfy, Jill says. And she walks into the kitchen and works a lighter against a Newport. Then she asks if Wade wants a Scotch and water. She says, It's all Randy ever drank. He left bottles of the stuff.

Randy is her second ex-husband. He works on plumbing for a living.

As Jill leans against the edge of the counter and pours the drinks, Wade goes to an earth-toned recliner next to the couch occupied by Temmy. The 65—inch OLED television overwhelms the small area. Cartoon Barbara is in the passenger seat of some fictitious automobile resembling a red Ferrari. Soon Jill moves across the linoleum with two glasses of Scotch and water. Too much water for Wade's taste, but he doesn't mention anything. Jill plops down beside her daughter, crosses her legs, rattles the cubes in her glass. Her bra strap is askew of her tank and twisted several times over her shoulder. It doesn't seem to bother her. The television is still going loud and the three of them sit there, watching Barbara. Jill begins to suck on her drink. When she drains the glass, she lights a cigarette.

Wade scratches an irritated bump on his forearm and says, Seems like a bad summer for mosquitoes. Then he slides to the edge of the recliner and leans forward uneasily. He raises his voice and says, Hey, Jill, whatcha think of my new haircut?

Huh, says Jill in her smoker's voice.

My haircut, how do you like it?

Jill gives Wade a lingering look before saying, Looks like the way Randy used to wear his hair. You know. . . kinda slicked back to cover his bald spot.

Wade remembers Jill and Randy at the bowling alley. That was two years ago when Wade had a wife, and Jill and Randy were still going through their rough spot before he ran out on her for good. Wade thinks hard, but he can't recall anything about Randy having a bald spot and he thinks Jill's remark is intended to make him uncomfortable, upset his balance.

Just then, some older guy appears in the window behind the television. He takes the cigarette from his lips, cups his tattooed hands on the window, presses his face close to the glass. Jill goes over and slides the window open. It's Alicia Marie Sanchez's husband, Eddie. He tells Jill that Alicia Marie's car overheated on Highway 17 coming back from visiting their grandson, Gil, in Watsonville.

Here's the thing, says Eddie, Gil's meeting up with her right now to fix the car. So it won't be long before she gets up and running and on the way here.

THE SUN SINKS BEHIND Montebello Ridge and the sky shimmers in afterglow. Jill becomes too hungry to wait for Earl's Spit Broil and decides to rustle up some food while they wait for Alicia Marie. While she puts Mini Corn Dogs in the oven, Wade goes quickly down the hall to the bathroom. When he flushes, water seeps from under the base of the toilet bowl and pools up on the linoleum. On the wall, the silver hand towel ring is empty of towels. Wade drops to his knees and looks in the small cabinet under the sink for a washcloth or towel or some sort of wiping rag. He looks behind the hair flat iron and hairspray, and that's when he sees a pair of pliers and a cardboard box full of toilet paraphernalia: flappers, wax rings, levers, floats, lengths of chain—the works.

Immediately Wade thinks of Randy and Randy's plumbing work—the trouble shooting and creation of things. God knows, he himself does not have the fortitude to do something like plumbing. He has a job in a wrecking yard. He operates the crane and big magnet—picking up vehicles, dropping them down. He's a destroyer. So it is no surprise to him that he had destroyed his marriage to Margie. These things he thinks about as he retrieves a hand towel from the far corner of the cabinet and works it over the pool of toilet water.

Wade hangs the towel on the silver wall-ring, and then hurries down the hallway. As he approaches the living room, he sees Jill and Temmy on the couch, leaning into each other, whispering. He doesn't hear the exchange of words, but he has the terrible feeling they're talking about him, and that Jill is somehow doing him a favor with her dates. He enters the room. Jill looks at him, lifts her glass, rattles the cubes.

She says, How about another refresher?

Wade points down the hallway and says, You know you got a leaky toilet.

Yeah, it's been like that for weeks. Randy says he'll fix it on a day he stops by to pick up Temmy. But every time he's here, he's got some stupid excuse for not doing it. Anyhow, you want a drink or not?

Ah, I guess so. Sure, twist my arm.

Jill gets up and makes for the kitchen. They'd already had four drinks and her feet wobble a little in her pumps. She gets the fifth of Scotch and pours the drinks.

Jesus, she says to no one in particular, I hope nothing bad happened to Alicia Marie. All this worrying is going to push me to an early grave.

Wade leans back in the recliner and says, I'm sure she's okay. Nothing to worry about.

The Barbara movie ends and Temmy mutes the television. She grins. Putting a fake cell phone next to her ear she says, Yes, that's right. He doesn't have a very chill car. . .

Jill comes into the room and hands Wade his drink.

Okay, Buttercup, it's time to go to your room and play until Alicia Marie gets here.

But, Mom, I'm right in the middle of an important call.

Well, finish it in your room. And you can take the bag of Oreos with you if you want.

Jill plops onto the couch and begins killing time with small talk while the Mini Corn Dogs bake. Her sentences flow into each other, as if someone unscrewed her head and let her thoughts splash out onto the area rug. She tells Wade she used to live in Amarillo, in an apartment off Highway 66. For years, she worked at a helicopter assembly plant and before that at a drive-in movie place. She tells Wade that Amarillo is smack dab in the middle of the Texas Panhandle. She says, It's the High Plains, real flat and windy. And when the wind decides to blow in from the southwest, you could smell the cow poop floating in from Hetford, 45 miles away. People would say, There's the smell of money.

The oven buzzer goes off. Jill moves into the kitchen to get the Mini Corn Dogs and Wade polishes his drink. He says, Mind making me another.

WADE JERKS AWAKE and rubs his eyes with tight fists. His head hurts, a hangover is already setting in. He sits up and focuses on the room. The clock on the wall says it's half past one. Jill is on the couch, sleeping sitting up. In his lap, a paper towel cradles a single Mini Corn Dog. He wets his lips and pops the dog into his mouth. Then he gets up and looks out the window behind the television set. It's dark and streetlight glow spanks the aluminum mobile home roofing. Music is still coming from the mobile across the street. The edges of the mobile are now lit up with tiny white Christmas lights. Wade doesn't see anyone, but he hears laughter coming from inside.

Turning away from the window, Wade gets the remote from the coffee table and settles into the recliner. He points the remote and flips through the television channels. The weather report is on. He sips his drink and begins to relax. There are high winds in Amarillo. He thinks about Jill and doesn't blame her for moving away from that place. No, he says aloud, I don't blame you at all.

Wade suddenly has an urge to urinate. On the way to the bathroom, he peeks into Temmy's room. The night light upon the bureau shows her sleeping on top of the covers, curled up with a stuffed Chihuahua. He closes the door, and then continues to stumble down the hallway.

Now the leak under the toilet bowl is worse. When he flushes, water spreads across the floor and pools up where hallway carpet meets linoleum. Suddenly Wade remembers the fix-it kit under the sink and he thinks: If what's his face can do it, how hard could it be. And he thinks, right now if he walked in here I'd take a swing at him for leaving Jill when her condition took a turn for the worse.

Wade wants to hang out with Jill for a long, long time. He wants someone to share new memories with. But he feels he can do nothing for her that she can't do herself.

After returning to the kitchen to fix himself a drink, Wade gets down to business. He shuts down the water valve, flushes to drain the tank reservoir, and uses his empty tumbler to bail the remaining water from the toilet bowl. Then he gets the pliers and goes to work on the nut at the base of the toilet. But he forgets the *lefty-loosey* rhyme and his dyslexia gets the better of him. He turns the nut the wrong way, snapping the bolt, cracking the porcelain base. He learns from his mistake and the second nut comes off without a hitch. Bending at the knees he bear hugs the toilet and pulls it away from the vertical bolts, wax ring, and drainage pipe. The next thing he knows he's peeling back the linoleum. Right away, he notices the extent of the damage. The particle wood floor is wet and rotted. He presses the flat of his hand against the wood. That's when his hand pushes completely through the floor. And when he takes a close look, he can see dirt down there. Suddenly he becomes conscious of germs and the bathroom begins to feel like some god-awful cave and claustrophobia sets in. He shoves the hand towel into the mouth of the sewer pipe and thinks: To hell with it, I'll finish things in the morning.

IN THE KITCHEN, Wade closes the window blinds and pours himself another Scotch over two cubes—no water. Then he goes out to the living room. Jill is still on the couch, laying down with a pillow under her head. Wade lowers his head over her face and stares past her thick make-up. He sees lines around her mouth and sagging skin under chin and neck. Her cardboardness falls away, betraying a face set with worry, betraying the toll of bladder cancer and the scraping the doctors put her through the previous year. She's a survivor, he thinks. And he knows she's out of his league—just as she's out of Randy's league. This he knows.

The Vacuum Cleaner

Cleat used his fingers to comb back his thinning silver-gray hair, then leaned forward in the kitchen chair and rubbed Vaseline over the open blister under his right knee, where his leg should have been. After five skin grafts, his skin was as thin as cigarette paper. He inspected the blister, put a silicone liner over his leg stump, strapped the prosthetic into place, pulled up his trousers and slipped into his sneakers.

Elvie said, "Why so quiet over there?" She was bent over a skillet, using a spatula to work a packet of Hamburger Helper into ground beef and macaroni. "Why so quiet?" she repeated.

"Just thinking."

"About Matthew's visit?"

Elvie was short and heavy, but she had a happy-go-lucky bounce to her step and her eyes beamed with affability. She wore a blue muumuu flecked with Hibiscus flowers, a gift from her book club friend after visiting Honolulu. Cleat knew it was a big day for her. Their son didn't come around as often as she wanted.

"No," he said then added, "Not everything revolves around Matt, you know."

"So what are you thinking about?"

"About work, if you really need to know," he told her.

"Thought the boss told you not to worry, that you're safe on account of your seniority."

"Sure he did. But I called him while you were at the grocery store. Called him and told him I wanted out."

"Cleatus, you didn't!" She put down the spatula. "Are you out of your mind?" she asked.

"Elvie, work is killing me. I can't do shipping and receiving anymore. I can't pick up and carry another box. If they're willing to give me severance to find another job. . . well then that's okay with me," he said. Then he told her he'd been talking to Buddy over at *Big Shots*. "Been talking to him on and off for the past five months," he said, "keeping my iron in the fire in case something opens up."

"And what are you planning to do for Buddy Macon? Drive one of them big limos?"

"There you go," he said.

"You're kidding?" Elvie's eyes narrowed. "I can't tell if you're kidding or not," she said.

"Couldn't be more serious. Buddy gave me the lowdown. He's going to let me drive the neighborhood, you know to get some practice, get the hang of it all. And as soon as I get my Chauffeur's license he'll start me out at fifteen an hour."

"So he gave you a job?"

"Ah, no, not yet. But I'm expecting to get a call at any moment."

Elvie shook her head. "I just don't see how you could have done something like this without discussing it with me first," she said.

Cleat glanced at the clock hanging above the sugar and flour containers—nearly five o'clock. "Look, could we discuss this later?" he said going to the entryway closet, where he picked up the vacuum cleaner canister in one hand, put the connecting hose around the back of his neck and used his other hand to pick up the vacuum head. The machine was light and Cleat easily carried it to the carpeted hallway leading to Matt's old room. He turned it on and got to work, carefully moving the suction up close to the baseboards, letting the airflow get the spots that collect most of the loose dirt. He was about to make another pass along the baseboard when a sharp snapping sound startled him. The beater brush stopped rotating.

"Shit," he said, "broken belt."

"What's that?" Elvie said from the kitchen.

"Damn belt broke again," he said as he hurried past Elvie. In the kitchen, he got a bottle of olive oil, a butter knife and two rubber bands from the asparagus bundle. He used the knife to turn the four screws away from the base bar. Then he removed the broken belt and stretched the two rubber bands over the rotating rod and base. It was a tight fit, but he managed the job. Before screwing the base bar into place, Cleat dribbled a bit of olive oil over the appropriate spots.

"There," he said, placing the knife in the sink and the oil in the cupboard. "I think that'll do her. But I don't think them bands are going to last long enough for me to do the upstairs."

"I don't care about the upstairs," Elvie said. "I just want the downstairs to be ready for Mathew's visit."

After a long pause Cleat said, "Sweetheart, I know you don't agree with me, but I wish Matt weren't staying the night. I trust that kid about as far as I can throw one of Buddy's limousines."

Elvie raised her brows. "Cleatus!" she said.

"I'm not ashamed to say it," he said. "Every time that kid rolls into our lives the money in my wallet has a tendency to disappear."

Elvie opened the oven door and used the spatula to gently turn each fry. "I think you need to talk with him, get down to the problem, find out why he does the stuff he does," she said.

He told his wife it was too late for things like that. "Somehow he got off on the wrong side of the tracks and now he's got some kind of what-have-you-done-for-me-lately attitude," he said. "And that's all there is to it."

A knock at the front door made Cleat leave the vacuum cleaner in the hallway and hurry to the kitchen window where he pulled aside the curtains and leaned over the sink faucet. Parked against the curb in front of his house was a run-down Cadillac Eldorado convertible with new-looking Goodyear radials. He let the curtains fall back into place.

"It's him. Matt's here," he said.

Elvie ran her palms over her muumuu, smoothing the wrinkles that had bunched up around the waistband of her girdle. "Cleatus Alan Holt," she said, "like it or not he's your son. So please behave yourself." Then she hurried from the kitchen to the entryway.

Cleat heard the front door open. Then voices.

"Mathew!" said Elvie. "It's awfully good to see you."

Matt laughed and said, "Hi Mom."

"How was your drive down?"

"Fine Mom. Fine."

"Well, let me look at you." There was a pause, then, "My, my, you're becoming more handsome each time we see you."

"You look great too, Mom. Hey, is that the dress Mrs. Bronkhorst gave you?"

"Along with three cans of Macadamia nuts," she laughed.

Cleat drew a deep breath and went to the entryway in time to see the exchange of hugs. He saw his son's two muscular legs sticking out from under his shorts and his body pressed against the muumuu. The scene looked strangely indecent to him. He didn't know why, but it did.

Matt said, "Hey Pop."

"Hi Matt," Cleat said uneasily, edging around his wife, reluctant to shake his son's outstretched hand but doing so anyway.

Elvie clasped her hands together and brought the tips of her thumbs to her chin. "Okay," she said. "Mathew, why don't you come in and put your bag in your old room? Just take those boxes off your bed and put them in the closet. Then wash up. Supper's in five minutes."

"Alright," Matt said as he picked up his duffle bag and headed down the hallway to his old room. When he came upon the vacuum cleaner he paused and tilted his head. "Hey Pop," he said, "thought you got rid of this piece-of-crap years ago."

Matt went into his room and shut the door.

Elvie turned toward Cleat. "Don't let him wind you up," she said.

Cleat stepped outside. The mid-afternoon breeze coming off the Stockton delta had calmed. The July air was hot and stagnant and felt heavy against his skin. Heat waves shimmered above the pot-holed road. There were no neighborhood sounds, just the metallic clanging in the nearby freight yard as railroad cars were loaded and unloaded and engines were fueled and serviced in the roundhouse. He leaned against the porch railing, pulled a match across the paint-flecked wood, lit a cigarette. Past the burning tobacco was the smell of fries coming from the kitchen oven.

CLEAT SAT ALONE at the head of the dining room table, waiting for his family to join him. Elvie had laid out their crochet lace tablecloth, a project her grandmother had done while convalescing from tuberculosis. For crying out loud, he thought, there's no need to spruce things up with the special occasion stuff. His body tightened.

Elvie and Matt carried the prepared food from kitchen to table. Elvie set down a bowl of fries and a bowl of ground beef and macaroni. Then she sat and draped a napkin over her lap. Her manner was cheery.

"It's lovely to have you home again," she said to Matt.

Cleat gave Matt the once-over. "So how's life these days at the mini market?" he asked.

Matt set down the sliced tomatoes and cottage cheese then took a seat. "Guess I haven't told you," he said. He began picking at the lace tablecloth with his forefinger. "Don't actually work there no more. There was a shooting a few weeks ago. One of the night clerks got shot in the chest so I quit."

"What on earth?" said Elvie. "Are you alright?"

"Mom, it had nothing to do with me."

"So where you working now?" Cleat wanted to know.

"A carwash."

"A carwash! Christ's sake, Matt, wouldn't you say it's about time you got a decent job, a job with some sort of promise?"

Elvie said, "You sure you're alright?"

Cleat said, "If you're not careful all your money'll run out. Then what?"

Matt seemingly agreed. "I could sure use a good job," he said. "Pop, you always get good jobs and I'd sure like to get the kinds of jobs you seem to get. Seems like I have rotten luck when it comes to jobs."

Cleat thought back to his old job, the one before he got into shipping and receiving—the sawmill job. In those days saws were powered by steam and the room temperature regularly shot up to one hundred-fifty degrees and the men made good use of wall-mounted salt tablet dispensers. One day the heat had gotten to him. He'd sweat all the moisture from his body, there was nothing left to give, his hamstrings were a mess of cramps. He remembered being lightheaded as he climbed atop the conveyor belt. He remembered kicking at a log, trying to clear the jammed saw blade, trying to get things working again. Kicking and kicking and all the while feeling as if he was floating high above the floor, high above the machine, which cut logs into dimensional lumber. He was delirious but he had enough sense to know he would never in his life have the same sensation. He felt at peace with everything, even as he observed the log jumping free and the blade whirling through his leg below the knee.

Cleat pointed his cigarette at his son. "Son, since the day I was born," he said, "I've never seen anyone as lazy as you. I'm not kidding. With your what-have-you-done-for-me-lately attitude, you've got yourself stuck in some kind of lazy streak like nobody's business." Then he preached the Bible to Matt, something he hadn't done in years. He said, "Boy, don't you know that man is born to labor as the bird is to flying!"

Elvie said. "Hey you two, remember me. I'm asking if anyone wants ketchup."

"Christ, Elvie! You know we all want ketchup," said Cleat, spooning the hamburger and macaroni onto his dish. "So why are you asking?"

Matt broke in. "So what's new around here?" he asked.

Elvie said, "The Hanley's got an in-ground pool. But they never invite anyone over to swim."

"What do you mean?"

Ash from Cleat's cigarette dropped into his dish. He became gruff. "Just like she says," he told Matt. "He's got a pool and never invites no one over. Doesn't even invite Stuart Blandford. And Blandford's the one who called the fire department the time Hanley's garage caught fire from his water heater."

Elvie said, "Anyway, your dad gets angry every time he hears splashing next door."

Cleat hunched over his dish. "Christ," he said. "Can we just eat and save the commentary for later."

They ate in silence until Cleat lit a cigarette and got up from his chair. "I'm going to see what's on TV," he said, and he went into the living room.

CLEAT PUSHED HIMSELF DEEP into the overstuffed couch pillows and used the clicker to find the news. The station was broadcasting a special two-hour report. Municipal employees were being told to take a hike because Congress had shut down the government.

Elvie came into the room carrying a plastic container of blackberries. "Yesterday I went down to the vacant lot behind Wal-Mart and picked nine bags worth," she said.

"My God, what a mess." Cleat said to her as she gave him the container. "None of those people have a conscience."

Matt sprawled back in the reclining chair, "What people?" he asked. "Who doesn't have a conscience?"

Elvie bent down close to Cleat. "Honey, why don't you give the clicker to Matthew? It's been a while since we watched one of his shows," she whispered.

"You must be joking," he said.

"Why not?"

"These idiots are whistling while things are burning to the ground and you want to give the clicker to Matt so we can watch who knows what instead of staying informed."

They became quiet in their TV watching. After a while, Cleat's mind drifted to a time when Matt was young, no more than seven years of age. They were in the bathroom and Cleat was using his forefinger and thumb to hold Matt's little finger. The fingernail was especially ragged and he had to clip it several times before getting a nice smooth curve. At the time, Matt's fingers were small and soft and frail.

When the program ended, Cleat stood up. "Well, that was a damn waste of time," he said. "I'm calling it a night. Elvie, let's go upstairs and hit the hay."

Matt said, "Thanks for letting me crash here for the night. Driving from Yreka to L.A. in one day would have been difficult. This is the perfect rest stop."

Cleat cleared his throat. "Forget it," he told his son.

Elvie went over and tapped Matt on the knee, gave him the clicker.

"You can watch TV for as long as you like. Make yourself at home," she said. Then she turned away and followed Cleat up the stairs to their bedroom.

CLEAT SAT ON THE CORNER of the bed and removed his prosthetic. He thought of his son's defiance as he peeled the silicone liner from his leg stump. With a hand towel he kept on the nightstand, he wiped the stump clean of sweat and liquid from his blisters. Then he put on his pajamas and slid under the bedcovers. Elvie was reading some book for her book club. When he eased up close to her, she put the book in her lap and looked at him.

"Why do you have to be so hard on Mathew?" she asked.

Cleat grunted. He could not remember a time when his son had treated them with respect. Respect, there was no respect for anything anymore. "Sweetheart let's face it," he said eventually, "we have a loafer for a son. I wouldn't treat a dog the way he treats us."

Elvie turned off the bedside lamp. The room darkened.

"He's young, he can change," she assured him.

"People don't change, Elvie."

"Please don't be that way."

Cleat rolled onto his back. The motion caused pain in the area of his missing limb. Sometimes his brain didn't know the mill had taken part of his leg, didn't know what to do with the signals passed on from the ruined nerves under his knee. He wanted to ask Elvie to massage the area of amputation. But he knew the request would weaken his position against his son.

He said, "I'm not expecting nothing from that boy."

Elvie insisted. "Just talk with him, okay?"

Cleat shut his eyes, tried to block the pain. "Alright," he said. "I'll try."

"Thank you," she said.

He scooted a little closer to her, felt the heat coming from her body. "Will you do some rubbing?" he asked.

"Sure," she said, and she sat up and blew warm air from her lungs into cupped hands before she began.

A SPLASHING SOUND made Cleat open his eyes. In the darkness his wife was an unmoving outline under the sheet. He touched her shoulder, rocked her body a bit.

"Hear it?" he asked.

"What's going on?" she asked. "Why'd you wake me?"

Cleat glanced at the clock atop the dresser. "It's nearly eleven-o'clock and that jerk-off Hanley woke me with his swimming."

"Good Lord, Cleatus," she said, turning away from him, "if it's bothering you, shut the window."

Cleat grabbed his crutch from its spot against the nightstand, struggled out of bed, hobbled across the room, opened the drapes. The moon was high and radiant and everything shone with a silver-blue brightness. Hanley's backyard was lit up: the neatly trimmed hedge against the far fence, the concrete patio and the swimming pool right there in the middle of it all. Cleat caught sight of a swimmer going up and down the length of the pool. Then his eyes widened with the crush of discovery. I'll be damned, he said to himself. He turned and whispered across the room to Elvie.

"Elvie!" he said, "it's Matt. Matt's swimming in Hanley's pool."

Elvie remained silent, unmoving.

For fifteen minutes, Cleat stood propped against his crutch, watching Matt splash along, and letting his mind race over the years of disappointment. When Hanley didn't come out and keelhaul his son, Cleat went to the nightstand and opened the top drawer. His wife stirred but continued to sleep. With care, he withdrew the address book. Then he retraced his steps to the window. His son was still at it, mechanically swimming away as if he were a wind-up bathtub toy: splash, splash, splash. By moonlight, Cleat looked up Hanley's number. He dialed. Next door, a lamp went on in the upstairs window and someone picked up the receiver. Cleat quickly hung up and waited for Hanley to recognize the situation. But after a few minutes the bedroom light went out. Cleat dialed again. This time the light remained off and the telephone rang and rang until the answering machine clicked in. "Screw it," he thought, and he got back into bed.

For a while, Cleat fussed with the bedcovers: pushing down the blankets, smoothing wrinkles in the sheet, getting comfortable. Perhaps he should call the police, report his son for trespassing, put the fear of prison into his blood. He glanced at the telephone and visualized Matt standing next to other men in a police lineup. "Yep," Cleat told the officer, "that's the swimmer."

MORNING LIGHT MEANDERED through sycamore-lined streets, continued over Hanley's pool and entered Cleat's window. It was a dim grey-blue light, but it was enough to rouse him from a restless sleep. He awoke feeling tired. His skull felt empty. Elvie had already rolled out of bed and was in the bathroom eagerly getting ready for the day. She loved her morning spit-baths: warm water, almond-scented soap, a clean hand towel. That was Elvie—a clean hand towel every morning.

For a moment he fell asleep again, but his wife's voice made him open his eyes.

"Cleat, are you awake?" she asked.

"Uh-huh?"

"How about a nice biscuits and gravy and sausage breakfast? How does that sound?"

"Sounds okay."

She lessened the flow of sink water. Her tone became serious. "Now I want you to remember your promise," she said.

He rolled on to his side and stared into space and thought of his defiant son. "What promise?" he asked.

"Don't go giving me that," she said. "The one we talked about last night."

"Oh, that promise."

"Now, Cleatus, I want you to make amends with that boy."

Cleat reached over to the nightstand and got a package of cigarettes. He lit up. "Just as soon as I finish my morning smoke," he said, "I'll go downstairs and give him a fatherly chat."

"Now I don't want any fighting, okay? Are you listening to me?"

"No fighting. I hear you," he said.

THE STAIRS CREAKED as Cleat made his way to the lower floor. In the hallway, he moved around the vacuum cleaner and gave Matt's room door a good hard knock.

"Hey Matt," he said.

When there was no answer, Cleat opened the door. Matt and his duffel bag were gone. Cleat went to the kitchen window, looked out. A dog was sniffing around the curb where the beat-up Cadillac had been. It's always the same old crummy thing, he told himself. Never in a million years could he have imagined that the milk from Elvie's breasts would nurture such a displeasing son. Just then, Cleat's brain went into motion. If he could get Elvie over to his side, then Matt would be hung out to dry. The house would become peaceful. Life would be a picnic, so to speak, he thought.

For a moment he stood motionless, looking at the hallway ceiling, anxiously listening. Sink water in the upstairs bathroom trickled into the drainpipe. Cleat picked up the vacuum canister, connecting hose and head. Then he went to the garage, where he flipped on the overhead fluorescents. The light was harsh and made his Vietnam-era Lincoln Continental seem whiter.

He moved quickly to the Lincoln, put down the vacuum and opened the trunk. Leaning over he placed the vacuum canister next to an old tackle box with a *Kiss My Bass* fishing decal on its lid. His forehead wrinkled with emotion. Sometimes in order to achieve a greater good, people found themselves having to do things harmful to others that are close. Honor be damned. Still, if his mother could see him now, he thought, she'd lay into him like nobody's business. How could you do this dreadful thing to your own son? And what about Elvie? How's she going to feel about all this? But his mother had died in Matt's early childhood. She had never known the years of grief his son brought to the family.

He was preoccupied with this thought as he leaned down and picked up the metal vacuum head. A loud cracking sound brought him back to things at hand. He had brought the vacuum head up hard against the taillight. Now red plastic shards littered the garage floor. Open mouthed he stared at the tiny pieces. In the bathroom above him the sink water stopped. The ceiling squeaked as Elvie moved out of the bathroom and walked over to the bed. "Son of a bitch," he said aloud. He quieted his breathing and listened. More squeaking as she moved from one side of the bed to the other, pulling up sheets, smoothing blankets, fluffing pillows.

Only a sense of resolving the family situation pushed Cleat into wild action. He put the vacuum head and hose in the trunk and shut the lid. Then he swept the plastic shards into a newspaper, folded the newspaper into a tiny square and threw the square into the trashcan. Sometimes his prosthetic dragged behind and he stumbled. But years of hobbling practice kept him upright.

IT WAS WITH AN ACHING LUMBAR and tousled hair that he went back into the house. As he shut the door to the garage Elvie came down the stairs and stopped on the last step. He looked at her hesitantly and, not knowing what else to do, stood there with his hands in his pajama pockets. Her hair was piled on top of her head and held into place with hairpins and her bathrobe seemed shorter than he remembered. Varicose veins stood out on both calves.

"Were you in the garage?" she asked.

"Nope," he said.

"Well," she said stepping into the hallway and heading toward Matt's room, "have you checked in on Mathew?"

"He's gone."

She peeked first into the room then down the hallway at Cleat. "Quit your fooling, now," she said, "is he in the shower?"

"I told you, he's gone." Cleat looked down at the recently vacuumed carpet. "No big surprise," he said. "No big surprise at all."

Elvie's face paled, nostrils widened. Her composure fell apart. "What do you mean?"

Now Cleat looked up from the carpet and made his eyes hard. "I mean while we were in our bed sleeping, our sorry-ass son took off without a note or anything. I'm telling you, that boy has gotten off on the wrong side of the tracks and he ain't never coming back."

Elvie's face became flush.

Suddenly Cleat said, "Hey, where's the Electrolux?"

Elvie stood there, looking as if she'd been slapped.

Cleat hurried over to the entryway closet, opened the door and moved his eyes over the photo albums and extension cords on the top shelf and the winter coats hanging from the hanger bar.

"It's not here," he said. "He took it. Matt took our vacuum cleaner."

Elvie went to the refrigerator and got a pitcher of orange juice. "Oh, stop that nonsense?" she said. "What could he possibly want with that broken down wreck?"

"He wants to hurt us. He knew we bought that thing on our first-year anniversary. It was the finest vacuum cleaner we could afford!" he yelled. "Okay, that does it, I'm calling the police."

Elvie set the pitcher on the counter next to the sink and began to weep. Cleat's eyes softened; no longer pleased with himself he went to her. Her skin was warm and almond-scented.

"My beautiful wife," he said. He touched her wet cheek with the edge of his pajama sleeve. "It's horrible you know," he mumbled. "If I turn Matt in, the bail money would come from my own damn wallet."

INSTEAD OF HEADING TOWARD the telephone on the kitchen wall Cleat went outside and sat down on a metal lawn chair on the front porch. He withdrew a cigarette from a pack he had taken from the kitchen counter, lit it, breathed the smoke. Dawn had yellowed the east and was creeping across the sky. He knew the neighborhood kids would already be under the iron bridge, fishing the Middle River as it flowed past Union Point Marina. Years ago, he and Matt had tied their own flies and had used them along that same slow moving stretch.

Elvie came out and leaned against the screen doorframe. Cleat stared at her, unblinking. Her piled hair had fallen to one side and she seemed to be trembling. Her hand twitched and twitched.

"I guess you're right. You've been right all along, all these years," she said. Then she lowered her voice. "What do you think about going vacuum shopping this afternoon," she whispered.

"Maybe we should wait until Buddy gives me a call. Don't you think?" he said, leaning forward and snubbing his cigarette hard into the porch boards. He watched the smoke blow away past the edge of the porch and over the shriveled rose bushes. Suddenly he was frightened of himself, of the things he had done. But a call from Buddy would fix everything. "Let's wait until Buddy calls," he repeated.

With a Dark Cloud It Starts

The front door blows open again. Mateo Jr. hurries to the entryway, leans out over the waterlogged porch, looks at the morning. Rain beats down hard and sideways from a sheet of gray clouds stretching from horizon to horizon. Leafless trees sway against sudden gusts like dancing couples. He shuts the door, returns to the family room where his wife, Rosa Margarita, is relaxing. She is in her mid-twenties with soft caramel-colored skin and a prominent bridge to her nose. She is wearing a heavy red cotton robe and is sitting in a chair in front of the TV, her bare feet are propped atop the coffee table. When Mateo Jr. comes into the room, she waves to him with her half eaten fried tortilla, and as she waves some of the salsa and cheese is shaken from the tortilla onto the wood floorboards.

Mateo Jr. says, "It's coming down like a cow pissing on a flat rock from forty feet up," His face is set with worry. "This area has never had a summer storm like this. I think we're witnessing something new."

He concentrates on the TV screen. A reporter in a rubber coat and tall rubber boots is having difficulty standing his ground next to a levee. He leans against the fierceness of the rain and wind and talks into a microphone.

Rosa Margarita pushes her long raven hair away from her face, looks up at him. For a few seconds Mateo Jr. scratches his angular cheek then he puts his hands in the front pockets of his blue jeans.

"Is the water level still rising?" he asks.

"Suppose to crest the levee within the hour."

"I hate Stockton. It's brought us nothing but trouble."

She says, "You're the one who wanted to live out here, out in the boonies. I wanted to stay in Sacramento. I had a good job in Sacramento and my family was just down the street. Remember?"

"Babe, we've been through this a thousand times."

"Admit it, you have a thing against my family and found a way to drag me away from them."

"Don't be silly, Babe."

"You know perfectly well it all started years ago, before we were married, ever since you overheard Papá asking if I was sure about marrying a Protestant. Now you and him have an unsolvable rift, just admit it."

"I'm telling you, there's no rift. And if there is, it's coming from him not me. Now come on and let's get packing."

She shakes her head. The light in her eyes becomes cold. "I'm not packing a damn thing. Do you hear me, Matty. . . not one damn thing!"

"What do you mean?"

"I mean," says Rosa Margarita, "I'm going to sit here and watch TV and finish my damn Chilaquiles."

Mateo Jr. cannot believe his ears. His head begins to ache. "Listen to me," he says, "this is a serious situation. A flood warning is in effect, an official notice of evacuation has been issued."

Suddenly Rosa Margarita leans forward and points to the TV screen. Aerial footage of a rural neighborhood comes into view. Rain pounds down upon everything—roofs, graveled road, barbed wire fences, small pastures.

"God Almighty," she says, "would you look at that!"

"Hey," he says, "that's *our* house!"

They stare at the aerial view of their home. They see neighbors scurrying through the downpour, packing their belongings into vehicles with steaming exhaust pipes and fast-moving windshield wipers. Now the camera operator works his lens and zooms into their fenceless backyard. A black Labrador is rooting around next to the irrigation ditch behind their house. The ditch is overflowing and the dog bounds through the water.

"And that's *our* dog," he continues.

An off-screen reporter says something about making sure your animals are safe. *This is no time to be lax*, the reporter says to the viewing audience.

"Come on," Mateo Jr. says, gazing at the wall mounted shadow box. "We have to hurry. At least let's gather up our collectibles and photographs."

She sits, silently watching the TV, silently watching live footage of their dog bounding around in the storm.

His eyes dwell on the wall-mounted shadow box, on the ceramic Day of the Dead skeleton bride and groom statue purchased in a Taos roadside shop during their first cross-country trip.

"Come on, Babe" he groans. "This stuff means a lot to us. I don't want to lose seven years of memories. Can we just get a move on it and pack?"

"Um, I'm afraid not," she says. "I'm too damn busy." She talks without looking up at him.

Outside, the dog begins to bark. While the dog barks, he stands there, looking at her. Finally, he says, "On second thought I'll start packing and you go and see what he's going on about."

"Heaven's sake, you're always telling me what to do."

Rosa Margarita swallows the last of her Chilaquiles and lights a cigarette.

Mateo Jr. looks toward the front door. "Wow, he is really loud. I don't think I've ever heard him so loud."

WHILE MATEO JR. IS TALKING, Rosa Margarita gets up from the chair and rushes across the family room and into the hallway. Hands in his pockets he follows her to the bedroom. With her long legs folded under her, she kneels in front of the bookshelf under the window and begins removing books from the shelves and stacking them into several neat piles on the floor.

"Hey," he says frantically. "What in the name of God are you doing?"

She bristles with annoyance and points to the wall space next to the closet. "If you must know, I'm moving the bookshelf over there and moving the bed under the window. I've always wanted the bed under the window."

"You're rearranging furniture now?"

"It's something I should have done when we first moved in. I shouldn't have let you talk me out of it. You're always talking me out things. You're always telling me what to do."

He ignores her outburst. "Please," he says, "will you go and deal with that idiot dog. Maybe there's something seriously wrong with him."

"Stop interrupting my work. I'm not going anywhere. I'm staying here and rearranging things. Things need to be rearranged."

Husband and wife become silent, and in their silence they hear the TV in the family room. The news anchor is saying that the storm front is weakening, floodwaters are receding, the county officials are now canceling their order for evacuation. Together they look out the bedroom window. The downpour has ceased but trees still move wildly in the wind.

A sudden howling gust blows open the front door. A cold earth-smelling wind enters the house, moves down the hallway, finds them in the bedroom. Then comes the patter of paws and the clicking of toenails against the floor. In the bedroom threshold appears the dog, mud covered, soaked to the bone. A baby skunk hangs from his mouth like a rag doll. The skunk bleeds and squeals and hisses and secretes the smell of rotten eggs.

While Mateo Jr. grabs the collar of his shirt and tugs it up and over his nose, Rosa Margarita finishes her cigarette and crushes the butt into an ashtray on the windowsill. "Okay," he manages to say through his shirt, "I can see you've got a lot on your mind. I'll deal with this. You go ahead and do your thing, Babe."

She pushes back her hair, glares at him. "Don't *BABE* me," she snaps.

He averts her eyes, and as he moves toward the doorway, the dog growls and shakes the skunk violently from side to side. Mateo Jr. withdraws his outstretched hand and holds back his vomit. His eyes water. His heart throbs. He turns to her for support. But her attention is now fixed upon balancing *One Hundred Years of Solitude* on top of *A Field Guide to Western Butterflies*; going about her business as if the stench from the skunk and the coldness from the open front door were miles away.

Gradually understanding comes to him. Somehow, he has stopped making a difference in her life, and with this understanding a desire to lash out.

"And your Papá," screams Mateo Jr., "didn't call me a Protestant. He called me a damn Protestant! Do you hear me? A damn Protestant!"

105 Degrees Fahrenheit

LATE MORNING. JULY. Mitch sat at the counter in Freddy's Lounge, listening to the juke playing Tom Waits and watching bull riding on the muted television hanging from the ceiling over the beer taps. He was watching a small-town competition somewhere in Cheyenne when his girlfriend came in. She took the stool next to him. He looked at her; she wasn't bad looking for pushing sixty.

"Thought I'd find you in here," she said.

"So?"

"So the toilet's clogged in #27."

This he already knew. He was in front of the motel fixing a sprinkler head in the little area below the office window when he heard his girlfriend on the telephone taking the complaint.

Mitch said to her, "How do you know?"

"The guy rang me not ten minutes ago."

"Well, maybe it'll unclog itself."

"Lordy, Mitch, just go. We don't need no more complaints."

"Not worried about complaints."

"Come on, the owner is already pissed at us. Don't make matters worse."

The bartender came over. Mitch's girlfriend ordered a Bud.

"Bottle or draft?"

"Bottle."

Mitch emptied his Jack and Coke, ordered another, and then turned his attention to the television. When the next rider nodded his head, a guy with an oversized belt buckle leaned over the chute and nudged the bull with a cattle prod. Seventeen hundred pounds of bull jumped from the chute, spun left past a rodeo clown and whiplashed the rider all over the place. There he was, one hand gripping the braided rope, the other flapping around, hat flying, booted feet flailing. It was beautiful. Then the bull kicked the air behind him and bucked the rider to the ground. Five seconds. He was out of the running just like that. As he ran behind two clowns and climbed the fence, another rider sat waiting atop another bull.

Mitch said, "Would you look at that."

Mitch's girlfriend nudged him with her bottle. "C'mon Mitch," she said, "we need to keep this job."

Three years ago, sitting in the place that became their office, the owner had reservations about hiring them. He preferred married couples, they worked as a team, helped each other out with the managerial duties, he had told them. Mitch told him that they were to be married during the upcoming summer and the owner gave in.

Now Mitch said to his girlfriend, "Why can't you fix it? You've done it a million times."

"Because I got a few more things to get done before noon comes rolling around."

"Okay, okay," he said. He told her he would get to it after the next rider took a crack at it.

"Well, hurry up about it," she said as she took her beer to the end of the bar where she sat down in front of a machine that took quarters in exchange for games of solitaire.

At the same time Mitch finished his Jack and Coke, Downtown Dan came up to him. Downtown Dan made Mitch drink shots of Wild Turkey until he thought he would vomit. After two doubles, Mitch got up off his stool and hurried to the bathroom. It took a moment of shaking before he realized things were okay, he wasn't going to do it after all.

Bobby Stratton came out of the stall next to him. "Hey peckerwood," he said. Then he asked if Mitch wanted of go bluegill fishing at Stevens Creek Dam sometime soon."

"Sure, Bobby," he said.

"Hey, remember what happened last time?"

"Sort of."

"That was fucking funny, man."

"If you say so," Mitch said. Then he said, "I'll be at your place tomorrow morning—six o'clock sharp."

"That's cool, man," Bobby said as he went back into the stall.

NOW MITCH'S BRAIN RECEPTORS wanted more nicotine. He decided to go outside and have a cigarette. Moving through the half-light of the bar, he noticed Downtown Dan. He had finished his last double shot and was leaning over the pool table, lifting the rack from the triangular arrangement of balls. As Mitch walked by, Downtown Dan lifted his head and pushed his sunglasses down his nose. He asked Mitch if he wanted to shoot some. Mitch told him first things first; already he had a cigarette between his lips. He opened the door. Behind him, he heard the cue ball crack the solids and stripes every-which-way.

Outside, the wind gusted through the strip mall parking lot, hot and dry. Mitch worked on his cigarette and closed his eyes against the late morning sunlight. During recess in grammar school, Mitch and Robert Foster used to lie on their backs in the mustard field at the edge of the school lot and let the sun bake them. With eyes shut, they pretended they were in suspended animation, like astronauts in those '50s science fiction motion pictures they watched. Many times, they ignored the school bell and suffered detention because of it. They valued those moments of escape and wished they could have stayed in suspended animation forever, let the world with all its problems go by. But when the time came, they both went to Southeast Asia. In Vietnam, they became very close. But they were not so close anymore.

Turning his face from the sun, Mitch opened his eyes. Across the street, a girl in a tank top, baggy shorts and high heels loitered under a light bulb rimmed marquee announcing ALL NUDE DANCERS. When she noticed him, she tapped her index and middle fingers against her lips.

"Hey, Mitch," she yelled.

Mitch went to the avenue and made it through a break in the traffic. He handed her a cigarette. She put the cigarette between her lips and he lit it. She was twig-like with skin that pinched the angles of her cheekbones. They went nearer to the building wall, giving elbowroom to some crazy-looking man passing by. The heat of the wall was uncomfortable on the back of Mitch's neck and arms. He knew he had sweat rings on his t-shirt under his arms. But he didn't care.

He said, "How's things going?"

"Work, work, work," she said, "and still I'm barely making enough to pay the bills."

Then she told him that she had been filling in for some girl who had broken her ankle.

Mitch listened to her talk about other things while he watched the traffic go back and forth. Some of the passing drivers saw her and whistled or yelled things out their windows. After a while, she dropped her cigarette to the concrete and jerked her chin toward the door under the marquee. Her eyes were red-rimmed and looked sore.

She said, "I better be getting back."

"Well Trinity," he said, "it's always nice seeing you."

"Why don't you come in for a while? Watch me dance."

"Love to," he said. "But a bunch of maintenance stuff is waiting for me at the motel."

"Bummer."

"Yeah, the owner's really coming down on us these days."

"Well, you got to do what you got to do," she said.

MITCH HELD THE DOOR OPEN for Trinity and followed her into the club. They walked into a foyer postered with photos and names of coming attractions. Then they went through a curtain of stringed beads and into a large room lit by a dim white light over the bar area and by shimmering violet and green lights upon the stage. The music was loud. A dancer with long blond hair leaned forward and shook her shoulders over five young-looking servicemen staring up at her. Mitch watched her as he walked up to the bar.

Trinity touched him on the shoulder. "I'll be right back," she said, and she walked to a darkened corner and went into a room.

Mitch ordered two shots of Wild Turkey from the girl behind the bar, and then turned toward the stage. He wasn't thinking of the clogged toilet in #27 anymore. Before the dancer had finished her set, Trinity returned wearing a G-string and black mesh crop top. She sat beside Mitch and swallowed her shot.

"This DJ is no good," she said, "I can't stand the sight of him. Every time I get up there he plays Madonna. I hate Madonna. I told him that if he keeps messing with my tip money he'll find himself being scraped all over the sidewalk by my boyfriend. That should fix the problem, don't you think?"

Mitch said, "I can't stand Madonna either."

The DJ's voice came over the speakers. "Okay that was Jade for your entertainment," he said. "Be kind to her in tips. Now you're in for a treat. Up next is the fabulously fabulous, one and only: T R I N I T Y ."

There was some loud transition music with plenty of bass while Jade and Trinity traded places. Trinity walked up there, singularly focused on tip money, looking confidently at the servicemen. She wrapped a rag around the pole, wiped it down, tossed the rag onto a chair in the shadows. The transition music ended and some Madonna song came on. But Trinity didn't miss a beat, didn't even look over to the DJ. She was a true professional through and through.

Mitch ordered a Jack and coke. There was a television on top of the fridge and he started watching some car race. Then he remembered about the bull riding and asked the bar girl for the remote. He flipped to the channel just in time to watch a rider come flailing from the chute. The rider was out of rhythm with the bull. Three quick seconds and he was down hard, unmoving. Clowns distracted the bull while medics came into the arena.

It did not take long before Jade came up to Mitch. She was an older Jade than the colored lights had let on. Right away, she wanted him to drop money on her.

"You want go to the V.I.P. room where I can use your body as a jungle gym?" she asked.

"No thanks."

"Shit," she said.

She had been dancing for twelve years and now felt she should find a different job because of her fading looks. Mitch stared at her while she talked. Perspiration dotted her upper lip.

She said, "I got to find something quick, this place is destroying me."

"Listen," he said, "sometimes you need a cattle prod to get things moving."

"What the hell are you talking about?"

"I think you know what I mean," he said. But he had no idea what he meant.

Jade began to blink a lot. Then she told him to fuck off and gave him the finger before leaving.

One of the servicemen came up to the bar. "You sure put her ass out of joint," he said to Mitch.

"Yeah," said Mitch, looking at the man's uniform. "You just return or heading out?"

"Being deployed next week."

Mitch said, "Well, how about letting me buy you a drink or three?"

They slugged down several beers and talked about women and cars and making things with their hands and not worrying about things you can't control. They drank and laughed and talked until neither of them had anything more to express.

Mitch put out his hand. He wanted to say something about pain and tragedy and courage and sacrifice and death. Instead, he said, "Well, you and your buddies stay safe out there. You, you hear?"

"Yes, sir."

They shook hands.

Mitch gave the serviceman's hand a good squeeze before letting go. "Thanks for your service, man. Catch you on the flip side," he said.

The serviceman nodded then drifted off to his companions. Mitch turned around on his stool and looked up at the television.

He watched the screen for a long time. He switched from Jack and Coke to Wild Turkey shots, and then switched back. Bull riding ended. Something else came on, and then a rerun of the Iditarod started up. At one point, Mitch balanced himself on the stool and removed his left sneaker and sock. His foot itched and he couldn't rid himself of the feeling. He pointed to his foot and asked the bar girl if she could see some sort of rash or something. The bar girl told him to put his shoe back on.

The night shift girls began to straggle in. Mitch hardly noticed them.

MITCH WAS DIZZY when he walked across the club floor. He staggered outside and went to the edge of the sidewalk. It was a warm night with no breeze. A couple passed him, and he could hear them talking about how unusually hot it had been recently. He lit a cigarette and worked his lungs against it for a moment while looking at the blur of headlights and taillights. Down the avenue, the huge motel sign was not lit up as it should have been. And as he stumbled across the avenue, making his way to Freddy's Lounge, he wondered why his girlfriend had neglected her duties.

Inside Freddy's, his girlfriend was sitting in front of the same machine, banging away at the buttons, playing solitaire, looking boozy, talking to some guy who had his arm around her shoulders. She must have spent a fortune on that machine, he thought.

Mitch turned around and exited the bar. He was no longer the master of his coordination. His central nervous system was having difficulty passing information to his muscles. Using the side of the building as a stabilizer, he went down two doors to the Vietnamese restaurant. He went into the restaurant and stumbled past the rectangular fish tank. The owner, a tall Caucasian man with a weathered face, hardened eyes and gray hair down past his collar saw Mitch and headed to the refrigerator. Mitch found an empty booth, sat down, slid his knees under the Formica tabletop. No sooner had he leaned back in his seat than he was given a cold can of Ba Muoi Ba.

"Thanks, Bonzo," he said.

Bonzo said, "Any food?"

"Yeah. Gimme some. . . some. . . of that Goi cuon and a bowl of Bun Cha."

"You got it, man,"

"And bring me some chopsticks, okay? I want some goddamn chopsticks."

"Sure, Mitch. Chopsticks. I know you like chopsticks."

As he waited for his meal, Mitch listened to Marvin Gaye coming from the tape machine in the kitchen and tapped his fingers against the tabletop.

The wooden food tray arrived. Mitch started to eat, but he couldn't control the chopsticks; pork and rice noodles went everywhere. Bonzo knew the drill. He was there, exchanging the chopsticks for a fork.

Bonzo was with Mitch at the fall of Saigon. They were together on April 29, 1975, when the evacuation code went out over the radio. *The temperature in Saigon is 105 degrees and rising.* Then music came on. *I'm Dreaming of a White Christmas.* The code kicked off the helicopter evacuation. *Operation Frequent Wind.* That Bonzo, Mitch often thought, he would have enjoyed lying in the mustard field with me and Robert.

Mitch looked over his shoulder at Bonzo. "Hey man, my foot stinks to high heaven. I. . . I think I got me some of that damn jungle. . . jungle foot," he said.

Bonzo said, "Naw. We took care of that a long time ago. You're fine now, buddy." As he spoke, he gently patted Mitch's back.

"But," said Mitch, "I smell something terrible, terrible, awful and I can't get it out of my nose." Then he wiped the spittle and food from his lips, pushed the wooden tray to one side, put his cheek against the cold Formica tabletop and let his eye lids close.

Tall Are the Pines Far Away

Clothed in flannel pajamas, Clara was sitting at the kitchen counter when she heard a car come up the drive and into the carport alongside the house. Through the window above the sink, she surveyed the scene. The light of day was fading. Gray clouds moved across the Spokane sky, concealing the far away foothills crested with mature and hardy pines. In the carport, Mama slammed the car door and made her way around the rear of the station wagon. And as she hurried toward the front door she shivered and pulled her jacket tighter about her body.

The front door opened. Mama stepped into the living room from the front porch. A gusting wind blew past her, cold, oppressive. She closed the door, shed her jacket, hung it from one of the hooks on the wrought iron coat stand against the wall. Then she used her palms to smooth the wrinkles in the skirt of her blue and white waitress uniform. The back of her arms jiggled with the motion. "It's brass monkey cold out there, I'm telling you," she said.

Pushing her tangled red hair from her face, Clara looked anxiously into the living room, past Mama. She squinted at the laundry piled upon a couch under the window overlooking the front yard and street, and she began rubbing her forefinger over a thumb calloused from nineteen years of working the metal wheel of a cigarette lighter. "Before you even ask. . ." she said, "no, I didn't fold the clothes."

When Mama saw the pile, she let her purse drop to the floor. She said, "Listen, I'm glad to have my little rabbit living with me again, but when you moved back home you agreed to do the housekeeping."

For a moment Clara recalled her move back home. Just a while ago, she had lived downtown with Vance, in a tenement house squeezed between the Conoco station and the red brick building that was the Baptist church.

Mama said, "Are you listening to me, goddamit?"

Clara stared at Mama's scolding lips, the dull lipstick. Only then did she notice the split lower lip. Leaping up from the kitchen chair and moving quickly into the living room, Clara patted Mama's back and tried to get a closer look. She said, "What the hell happened, Mama? Is this Boyer again? I thought you quit that son-of-a-bitch!"

Mama's cheeks reddened. She jerked away from her daughter and went into the kitchen. "The hell with Boyer, this conversation isn't about Boyer," she said, "It's about you."

"Me?"

Clara watched Mama get a bottle from the fridge and pour a glass of wine.

When Mama returned to the living room she said, "What have you done for me lately? I mean name one thing you've done for me without me having to ask."

"I do lots of stuff around here."

"You can't even fold the clothes when asked."

"Mama. . ."

"What do you do all day long, huh? I'd like to know. Tell me."

"Okay, since you asked. . . I think! I sit around and tell myself that I'm not worthless and stupid and that the bad things that happened in the past aren't my fault."

Mama sipped her wine then became thin lipped. "Anyway," she said, "you were always a very lazy little rabbit."

"Oh, for fuck's sake, Mama. . ."

Mama took up a book of matches and a pack of cigarettes from the coffee table next to the TV and lit a cigarette. Then she touched the cut on her lip and looked at her fingertip. "From now on I want you to keep up with the chores," she said flatly, "And if you don't keep up, you're out." Then she went into the kitchen, got the bottle of wine and moved down the hallway to her room.

CLARA WORKED HER THUMB against the metal wheel of her lighter. She lit a cigarette then went over to the couch and began sorting the laundry: her clothes on one side of the pile, Mama's on the other side, towels and washcloths on the windowsill above the couch. Living with Vance, she thought, had been bullshit. She had thought they could make something together. Instead, he gutted her with whiskey and the back of his hand and his belt buckle.

Clara glanced up from the laundry. Through the window over the couch, she saw Mr. Brinkman. He was on the other side of the street, standing beneath the Z-shaped fire escape hanging over the entrance to his shop. He was a tall wiry man with a receding hairline. He stood there smoking, taking a break from his engraver's workbench. For quite some time now he'd been fool-headed over Mama. He was a decent guy, Clara thought, no hot number, but a decent guy. She was sure Mama would be receptive to him if Boyer weren't hanging around. Leaning across the couch, she banged on the window and waved to Mr. Brinkman, but he continued to smoke without acknowledging her. And as he stepped out of the wind to a spot alongside a window showcasing trophies, plaques and custom etched glassware, a tow truck pulled slowly up to the curb in front of Clara's house.

BOYER GOT OUT OF THE TRUCK, went to the edge of the driveway, stopped. His thick neck jutted up from his mechanic coveralls, leaving his skin exposed to the snapping wind. He started up the driveway, staring at the ground as he walked, stumbling from side to side. Clara wondered how he was able to operate his truck in this condition and she told herself that he would never make it to the top of the drive without going down. But he did make it to the top.

Clara hurried to the front door, stepped out onto the porch, shut the door behind her. The smell of oncoming snow was on the wind. She began to shiver. Her neck hurt with tension. Boyer looked at Mama's station wagon in the carport.

"I see she's home now," he said.

"She's sleeping."

"I swung by Alex's Café after she got off work. She seems tired."

"You hit her."

"She was tired and got a little snappy with me. But things are fine now. She told me to stop by after my last call."

Clara folded her arms below her breasts. "She don't want to see you no more, Boyer. She told me so when she got home."

Boyer moved up close to her, leaned forward, wavered on unsteady feet. The reek of alcohol was strong and stale. "I don't think so," he said. "She was a little out of hand, but I forgave her and now things are fine. So how about moving out of my way and letting me in out of this cold."

Clara became indignant. "Go to hell, Boyer," she said, "Mama don't want to see you no more."

"Now don't go pissing me off, little girl," he said. "Just move on out of the way and let me in."

"You ought to go away," she said. "You ought to go away now before I call the cops."

"I'm telling you, you'll be sorry."

"Please just go. . ."

"You'll be sorry if you don't let me the hell in."

Clara looked across the street at Mr. Brinkman. He stood at the entrance of his shop cupping a cigarette to his lips. He was looking down at the sidewalk and the wind took up the smoke coming from between his fingers and carried it past the window showcasing his engravings. She returned her attention to Boyer, looked at him closely. There was no decency in his face. It was difficult to believe Mama had any sociable feelings toward him at all.

Boyer staggered backwards and looked past Clara to the front door. "Irene!" he called. "Jesus Christ, Irene, let me in!"

Clara began rubbing her forefinger over her thumb callous. "I'll scream," she said, and she hollered into the wind to Mr. Brinkman. "Hey Brinkman!" she yelled.

But Mr. Brinkman was busy lighting another cigarette and showed no notice to her.

Boyer bent down and picked up the end length of garden hose that lay coiled in the mud next to the porch step. The threaded metal tip was muddy and a little bent.

"What are you gonna do with that thing?" Clara asked.

"I'm gonna beat your head with this if you don't let me in," he said coldly. "I'm gonna beat your head then I'm gonna find your mother."

THERE WAS A NOISE. Clara turned and Mama was standing there with wine-glazed eyes and tousled hair. And as they looked at each other, Clara heard the metal tip of the hose clank against the concrete.

"Now you see," said Boyer, "your mother's here to make things right. Aren't you Irene?" He pushed past Clara and stepped in close to Mama and hugged her with his thick arms and his cold breath went against her cheek.

Mama frowned. "What the hell's going on out here?"

"Nothing, nothing," Boyer said, and he led her into the living room and used his arm to clear the folded clothes from the couch onto the carpeted floor.

Mama looked confused. "You got some nerve coming around here," she said defiantly. But when Boyer told her to lie down, she stretched out on the sagging pillows and let him put an unfolded towel behind her head. Then she said, "I forget what we was fighting about." Her voice was hoarse, her tone fatigued.

Clara hurried into the living room. The pulse in her temples pounded as she yelled at Boyer. "Mister," she yelled, "I want you out of here right now!"

Boyer lay down on the couch next to Mama, half his body hung over the edge and it looked to Clara as if he would roll off onto the floor like two hundred and fifty pounds of chopped wood.

"Clara," Mama said, "Be a good little rabbit and get that bottle of wine from my bedroom and another glass from the kitchen."

For a moment Clara saw everything as a stranger might see it—the threadbare couch, the age-yellowed kitchen linoleum, the dirty walls, Mama's faded looks and high-strung loneliness. Slowly she realized she was looking out the window and that her eyes were locked with those of Mr. Brinkman. Then the moment was over. Mr. Brinkman dropped his cigarette to the concrete and went into his shop. She was left looking at Mama's split lower lip.

"Mama," Clara sighed, "you're messing up again. You can do better than this."

Clara twisted her hair into a bun and went down the hallway to her room. She shut the door, turned the lock into place and sat down on the edge of her bed. A hush filled the house and rain began to pitter-patter against the roof. Mama and Boyer came down the hallway and Boyer pounded on Clara's door a few times before going to Mama's bedroom. Mama stopped and spoke though the door.

"Don't go worrying, little rabbit," she whispered. "It's all been a horrible misunderstanding. Everything is fine now.

Boyer is nothing like your father so don't you go worrying yourself over nothing. We're both safe with Boyer around. Do you hear me? We're both safe."

The hallway floor creaked as Mama went to her room. Clara heard the bedroom door shut then she heard their laughter. The rain was now coming down hard. Gusting wind moved over the Monroe Street Dam, skimmed through the deteriorating neighborhood, rattled her window. She used her lighter, got a cigarette going. She reclined against the oak headboard, cold through her pajamas. Then she drew a breath from her cigarette and closed her eyes and held the smoke deep in her lungs until she felt hollow and a little dizzy before exhaling.

Extra Weight

RUTH WAS IN THE KITCHEN, making a ham and cheese sandwich for her husband's lunch and listening to the weather report coming from the television in the living room. When her husband came in and leaned against the counter, she pushed her gray-streaked hair away from her face then pulled her green bathrobe closer to her skin and tightened the terry cloth belt.

"Looks like the pass don't have no ice on it," she said.

"Yeah?"

"Yeah."

"Good. I hate putting them chains on a rig," he said while shoving the ends of his flannel shirt into his trousers.

Ruth saw the anxiousness leave her husband's face. The trek from their home in Sunnyvale California to Eugene Oregon was only five hundred fifty miles, but the pass just before Stateline often got nasty during bad weather.

"Well," she said, "when you get to Eugene give a call, okay?"

He went over to her and gave her arm a squeeze. "Okay," he said. "I'll give you a call from Eugene; let you know I got over the pass with no problems."

She recognized the tone in his voice. "You're not going to call are you?" she said. "How hard is it to call every now and then while you're on the road?"

"You don't understand the way it is driving an eighteen-wheeler all day long. Especially if black-ice is involved," he said crushing his cigarette into an ashtray at the counter edge. "I work hard and need to relax. That's why I forget to call."

"Well," she said, "this time I want you to call before you get to drinking with your truck stop buddies."

"There ain't nothing wrong with having a few pops to unwind."

"Listen," she said while halving the sandwich with a boning knife usually reserved for Steelhead her husband brought home during fishing season. "I got a whisper in my head saying today is going to be unlucky. So be nice to your old lady and call just this once."

With care, Ruth wrapped the sandwich in wax paper and placed it into a domed metal lunchbox. As she put a banana and a small can of apple juice next to the sandwich, her husband lit up a cigarette.

"Well, I've got a long trip," he said after exhaling a breath of smoke, "so I got to get going cause if I don't get there on time I'll lose my job."

Ruth frowned. "You're not going to lose no job," she said.

Her husband went over to the tile key rack next to the kitchen light switch and unhooked his keys. "Don't forget about them cookies," he said over his shoulder.

"Cookies? What cookies?"

"You know, for tomorrow's Halloween party over at Joyce's."

Ruth was supposed to make four dozen cookies and drop them off at Widow Joyce's place that afternoon. But she wanted nothing to do with the Widow. For quite some time she had been aware of the adultery going on between that woman and her husband. So it was a difficult thing to cope with, bringing cookies to her house.

Ruth got the lunchbox from the counter and went to the front door, where her husband was waiting.

"I would have remembered about them cookies," she said hoarsely.

"Make them spice punkin ones," he said, taking the lunchbox. "Everyone likes them spice punkin ones."

"Well," she said changing the subject, "I hope to Christ the weather holds. At least until you get home."

"Should be okay," he said. "Nothing I haven't handled before. So don't you worry none, I'll be back in time for the party."

Ruth stood on her tiptoes, stretched her five-three frame, kissed her husband's unshaven cheek. Her face twitched as the sharp bristles prickled her lips.

"I have to go," he said as he headed to the truck cab parked in the driveway.

She watched him step up into the cab. Then she closed the door, softly, knowing that in a matter of hours he would be far away from her.

RUTH DIALED THE OVEN to 350 degrees then poured herself a cup of coffee. In the living room, she turned off the television and turned the radio onto an oldies station. She moved across the room to the sliding glass door, where she stood sipping her coffee and watching a black bird preen itself atop a pyracantha bush. With rapid beak movements, it methodically groomed each glossy feather from base to tip, cleansing them of parasites. Then the bird stretched his wings as if to take a sunbath. But it was a cold and cloudy day, so the bird sprung into flight and disappeared over the fence.

The oven beeped, letting Ruth know it had reached the proper temperature. She drained the last of her coffee. Now she was ready. She was good at making spice pumpkin cookies. She'd been making them for as long as she could remember. It was something she had done as a little girl with her mother each year around Halloween.

After combining and mixing the ingredients, Ruth shaped the dough into little balls. Then she arranged them into four rows of six onto the cookie sheet and gently worked a fork against them, flattening and shaping the dough into the perfect size.

Now that the cookies were in the oven, Ruth had time to prepare herself for the day. In the bathroom, she disrobed and looked at herself in the long rectangular mirror above the sink. She moved closer to her reflection and saw a woman with sagging breasts and a constellation of moles and blemishes littering a soft tummy and with looseness around her cheeks and chin. At sixty-three, she looked in her late sixties. Suddenly she pictured Widow Joyce with her long natural silver fox hair, blue eyes and slender body. It was easy to understand why men found her attractive.

Ruth wetted a washcloth with warm water and worked it over her face and under her arms and between her legs. Then she went to the bedroom and retrieved a pair of elastic-waist briefs, a bra, gray sweatpants and an oversized Oakland Raiders sweatshirt.

Just as she finished dressing, the oven timer went off. Ruth hurried to the kitchen and quickly spatulaed the two dozen cookies onto a cooling rack next to the stove. Then she cleaned and greased the cookie sheet in preparation for the next batch. After putting the second batch into the oven, she suddenly became self-conscious of her appearance, realizing her current attire was unfitting for a get-together with the Widow. She needed something much fancier.

Controlled by this new urge, she returned to the bedroom closet and rummaged around. In no time at all she fetched a pair of navy-colored pants and matching blouse, which she believed gave her a slimming look. Then she framed it all with a long cable knit burgundy coat. Back in the bathroom, she worked some makeup over parts of her face. She finished up with an application of light red lipstick, something she had recently switched to because the darker colors were bleeding into the smokers' lines around her lips, giving her mouth a puckery look.

After the second batch had cooked and cooled, Ruth arranged the four dozen cookies onto a platter adorned with painted jack-o'-lanterns and green witches astraddle black brooms. As she stretched cellophane over it all, she let her mind drift. *Jesus, I have half a mind to let that bitch have my husband. That ought to teach her.* She smiled, and then lit a cigarette, picked up the platter and went outside into the blowing wind.

THE MID-MORNING AIR was crisp. Smells of dirt, oil and gasoline came up from streets wet from rain, reminding Ruth of when she first moved to the neighborhood. It had rained a great deal that year. Sewers backed up. Streets and sidewalks became flooded. She remembered her husband losing his job at the Ford assembly plant. That's when he got a long-haul trucking job. But the pay wasn't as good, so to save money they moved across town to this neighborhood. That had been a difficult year, she remembered.

As Ruth approached Widow Joyce's yard, she heard her name called out. She looked around and there on the opposite side of the street was Alice Clark, enjoying a morning walk and waving to her. Over her apple-body, Alice wore a loose-fitting gray sweatshirt and green sweatpants. Last year, Ruth suspected her husband of having a few sinful encounters with Alice. But no hard evidence was ever produced. Just rumors is all.

Alice made a beeline across the street, toward Ruth. "Hey, Ruthie," she hollered, "why you so dressed up?"

Ruth lied, telling Alice about a doctor's appointment she had later that afternoon.

"Nothing serious I hope," said Alice.

"Just a normal check-up," said Ruth. "You know," she continued, "one of them once a year things. Gives me a chance to dress up a bit."

With fingertips white from the chill, Alice gestured to the cookie platter. "Them for the party?"

"Yep," said Ruth, while making her way up the driveway to Widow Joyce's porch, Alice in tow.

Ruth knocked on the door and rang the bell.

Alice said, "I'm bringing a pumpkin shaped cheese ball made outta cheddar and cream cheese and some crackers."

The moment after Ruth knocked again, she heard some sort of commotion going on in the backyard. She stepped back, tilted her head. "You hear that?" she asked.

Both women clearly heard Widow Joyce's voice, loud, belligerent, filled with profanity. They hurried over to the wooden side gate and Ruth called out. "Hey Joyce!" she hollered. "Joyce, what's going on back there?"

Alice's face became tight with anger. "I wonder whose husband is back there with her?" she said as she unlatched the gate and made her way down the side yard.

THE TWO WOMEN hurried around the edge of the house and into the backyard. Widow Joyce was there by the poolside. She wore tight jeans and a button-down man's shirt with the top three buttons undone and no bra. With deep concentration, she worked a pole net back and forth through the dirty water, trying to skim something afloat.

Widow Joyce glanced at Ruth and Alice. She was drunk-faced and the cigarette between her full lips moved up and down as she talked. "Trying to get this little fucker outta the pool," she said.

The women moved closer and saw the focus of Widow Joyce's irritation, a dead black bird floating next to a cluster of brown and cracked sycamore leaves. They stood in motionless observation as Widow Joyce's body twisted and contorted with the effort it took to skim the net through the water. Again and again she worked the net. But each time the net neared the dead bird, the water current pushed it away. Blue veins rose from her forehead and neck and the cigarette fell from her lips to the edge of the pool where it continued to burn.

Suddenly the end of the long pole became jammed between patio table and chair. Widow Joyce looked at the end of the pole and swore. "Goddamned pole," she hollered and instead of finessing the jam, she mustered her strength and tugged the pole sidelong. With a grunt of surprise, her grip broke and she fell backwards. A small amount of blood appeared where her head cracked against the concrete.

As soon as Joyce hit the ground, Alice scrambled over and used the tip of her right shoe to roll the prostrate woman into the pool.

"Oh, shit!" Ruth whispered, looking at Alice in astonishment.

Joyce was motionless as she sank, face down, arms stretched out, legs spread eagled. Bubbles streamed up from around her silver fox hair. Then the bubbles stopped, and she rose slowly to the surface. When she broke water level, the two women looked at each other as the floating body nudged gently against the poolside.

Ruth felt lousy. She began to tremble. But Alice remained as clam as if she possessed justice on her side. With care, she adjusted the bobby pins, which held her hair in a small bun off her shoulders. As she fiddled with the pins, she talked.

"Can you appreciate what just happened?" she asked Ruth. "This was a golden opportunity, a once in a lifetime chance. And I took it."

Ruth shook her head. "I had a feeling, something in my bones, that this would be an unlucky day," she said as she sat down in the white plastic patio chair and crossed her legs. The coldness of the plastic went through her navy-colored pants, giving her goose bumps.

Alice came over and sat down too. She said, "Now Ruthie, the way I figure things, she had it coming. Always sneaking her way into the spaces between wives and husbands. Pissing on us, leaving us to feel like fools. Well, Ms. Naughty is not one to be envied now, is she?"

Ruth sat in silence as she worked the sleeve of her cable knit coat across her face, wiping away the sweat. Then she looked down at the platter resting on her lap. With care, she squeezed one trembling hand under the cellophane and retrieved a cookie. Be brave, she told herself and she found her voice. "Yeah," she admitted, "she's not to be envied now."

"I'm telling you, Ruthie, I got tired of feeling stupid," said Alice, reaching over and taking a cookie. "You know," she continued, "the other day I let my mind explore a bit and I got to thinking about the earth, about how heavy it's getting with all the people living on it now."

"What you getting at?"

"Well, I got to wondering how much more weight the earth could take before something bad happened."

"Like what?"

Alice looked at her cookie. Her green shadowed eyelids flapped a few times. "Hey," she said, "these are good. What kind are they?"

"Spice punkin."

"Well, they're damn good, so help me."

Ruth repeated herself. "Like what?" she asked. "What kind of bad things are you talking about?"

"Oh. Well, like our rotation or orbit getting all out of whack on account of extra weight."

"Jesus, Alice." Ruth's eyebrows arched. "Do you know how silly that sounds?"

"Walt says the same as you. But I've always been a big picture kind of gal. I like to work through things other people might ignore. You get my meaning?"

Ruth didn't know what Alice meant. So she sat in silence, legs crossed, chewing her spice pumpkin cookie, while Widow Joyce floated there against the blue mosaic tiles, her hair fanned out like some kind of silver frond, her wet shirt clinging to her slenderness.

Alice got up, lit a cigarette and went slowly to the edge of the pool. She bent over, looked at the floating body. "I got no room in my heart for people like her. Everyone ought to know their place in this world," she said. "And Joyce's place wasn't with my Walt." She straightened up and moved back to the plastic chair, sat down. "Now that she's dead and gone, I've brought back some dignity to my life and made the earth a little bit lighter. I'm proud of what I'd just done."

Wind blew in from the north, cold and vigorous. Ruth's hair blew against her face; she brushed it aside. A woodpecker flew over the pool, latched onto a telephone pole on the other side of the fence and began its rapid pecking for insects. Suddenly somewhere close by there was gunfire, a single shot then a car horn. The woodpecker flew away.

"Well," Ruth said absently, "seems like the cops are going to be in this area soon enough, so it's probably time to dial the emergency number."

"Wait a minute," said Alice, "swear to me you won't tell nobody about this?"

Ruth placed the platter of cookies onto the patio table.

"Sure, Alice. Cross my heart," she said.

"We'll tell the police that she didn't answer the front door so we came around back to knock on the slider. That's when we found her. Okay?"

"That's fine, Alice. I don't think anyone's going to think you murdered her."

Alice straightened up in her chair, pushed back her shoulders. "We did it together, Ruthie," she said quietly. "We both fucking murdered that home wrecker."

Ruth tensed for a moment. Then she scooted herself to the edge of the chair and stood up. On legs like dead weight, she left Alice and Widow Joyce and went into the house through the open sliding glass door. Her shoes squeaked across the linoleum as she moved toward the kitchen telephone. The surrounding countertop was crowded with bowls of wrapped candy, bags of orange and black streamers, bottles of liquor and a few stacks of plastic cups.

Ruth picked up the telephone receiver, dialed the emergency number. When the woman at the dispatch center got on the line, Ruth gave her name and Widow Joyce's address. Then she told the woman that she had just witnessed a murder.

"Are you sure, ma'am?" the woman asked.

"Yeah, I'm sure," she said. "It was Alice Clark who did the murdering. I saw it happen. I saw it happen and there was nothing I could do to stop it."

Small Voices

Truckloads of unwrapped and unlabeled cheese congest the driveway at Jackson & Woods Cheese Distribution Company. Drivers surrounded by window-fog sit in their cabs listening to the radio, reading the newspaper, drinking coffee, waiting in the violent sleet to unload their freight. Inside the warehouse stacks of collapsible boxes crowd the walls. Forklifts move hastily around. Loud noise from four conveyor belts resonates throughout. On each side of each belt, stand fifteen women—a mix of Hispanics and Caucasians. Every line worker on the payroll is there, working away.

Colleen is there, standing on one side of a conveyor. She wears earplugs and gloves and plastic booties. Her dark hair is bobby-pinned under a hairnet. A ten-pound block of shrink-wrapped cheddar moves down the line toward her. It could have been feta or Jack on the belt. It could have been a wedge or a round instead of a block. But today it is blocks of cheddar. She straightens the cheddar block, takes a label from her shirtsleeve, slaps the label onto the cellophane.

The cheese is warm from passing through an oven at the back of the conveyor. The oven seals plastic wrap around each block. Four ovens are in operation, one at the head of each conveyor, and so the room is hot—over ninety degrees. Colleen wears a wetted bandana across the back of her neck. The moisture cools her down somewhat. It's her mother's old bandana. Her mother had worked the line for years, until arthritis ruined her dexterity and put her on welfare.

Sweet Pea, the floor manager, walks past the line of conveyors and gives Colleen a menacing look. Sweet Pea and Colleen had been friends since the beginning of high school and during the eight years following. But recent events between Sweet Pea and Colleen's now ex-boyfriend ended their friendship.

Colleen straightens a cheddar block and gives Sweat Pea no attention. She likes to keep things moving without a hitch so she peels labels from a large roll and arranges them down the left sleeve of her shirt for easy access. Hours ago, she had flipped a switch in her brain, turned on autopilot. Her overworked body is now a machine. Her movements are quick and effortless.

Bend over.

Move gloved hands to conveyor.

Straighten cheddar block.

Transfer label from arm sleeve to cellophane.

Repeat.

Need more labels.

Peel labels from large roll.

Slap labels onto arm sleeve.

While her body moves, Colleen thinks about the upcoming evening and going with her friend, Wanda, to Tinseltown for a movie. Wanda came along nearly three months ago, after the fallout with Sweet Pea. They had met in the bread aisle in the local supermarket. Wanda has introduced her to a new set of friends and interests. Come spring, Wanda is going to show Colleen how to look under bushes and trees for morel mushrooms, show her how to dehydrate them for spaghetti sauce and quiche. Colleen now feels good about things, her insecurities stomped down by a newfound self-respect. She can be herself among new friends, share thoughts without fear of reproach. She is smiling with confidence again and no longer spends free time at the billiard room, as she did with her ex-boyfriend and his lumber mill friends.

Up the line from Colleen, blocks of cheese bunch together creating a traffic jam. She rushes over and helps to get things in order then returns to her post. Now she sees a cheddar block with air bubbles in the cellophane. She takes it off the line and smiles at the woman hurrying over to take the block to the cellophane staging area.

Bend over.

Move gloved hands to conveyor.

Working on the line at Main Street Distribution means working ten-hour shifts. Colleen doesn't mind. She considers herself lucky to have work. It's a good gig because of health insurance. But it's lonely work, despite being surrounded by people.

Move gloved hands to conveyor.

Straighten cheddar block.

She looks toward the end of the line. Two women work furiously, filling boxes with labeled cheddar blocks. They plastic wrap the boxes and stack them on a pallet. A rugged-looking man comes over with a pallet jack. He rolls the pallet across the floor to the shipping area.

SUDDENLY A MAN comes running. He waves his arms around like a crazy person and talks it up loud, yelling to anyone willing to listen. Several women remove their earplugs. Their faces screw up in astonishment as they catch onto the man's words. Here and there, they break from the line and hurry toward the rolled-up metal door on the far side of the room.

Colleen takes off her plastic gloves and follows two women. They hurry under the big rollup door and into the outside cold. A sheet of gray stretches across the sky. Northerly gusts blow the scent of freshly milled wood from one end of town to the other. Minutes ago, Colleen's short-sleeved blouse had offered her comfort against the heat from four ovens. Now the cold hits her, makes the skin on her arms and neck and chest look like freshly plucked chicken flesh. She hugs her breasts and shivers.

The conveyor belts are shut down, production stops. Everyone from the building is now outside. Truck drivers leave the warm nest of their cabs and join the workers. They stand in a ragged line, looking like cutout paper dolls. They watch the sky. An uncountable number of orange-sized things, dark and unmoving, whomp down onto roofs of houses, tops of cars, frozen pavement. And except for the percussive sounds made by the impact, all is quiet.

Colleen looks around the parking lot. Slowly she begins to understand what is happening. Birds are falling from the sky. There is no flutter of wings, just falling birds, dead in the air, dragged to earth by gravity.

Some people light cigarettes and stand by themselves. Others gather in small clusters and talk with frozen breath. Colleen stands by herself, blinking. Her plastic booties seemingly fastened to the ground. Never has she witnessed such an appalling sight. No longer aware of the cold, she cries.

Surprise wears away. People talk in excited tones.

Good Lord, I think they've stopped falling, at least I think they've stopped.

Bet there's a thousand of 'em out there, maybe more.

Never seen anything like it.

Oh, sure, strange things like this happen all the time. Why last week it was two hundred dead cows in Wisconsin; froze upright, feet stuck to the earth.

Groups of people hurry around with brooms and dustpans taken from the shop floor. Someone gives a push broom with thick black bristles to Colleen. She straightens her hairnet and works the broom across the asphalt, sweeping birds into small piles, clearing paths. Mostly it is starlings and red winged black birds. But there is a fair amount of robins too. After a while, a woman with a box of plastic gloves comes around. The woman tells her the birds might somehow be toxic so wearing gloves is a smart thing to do. Colleen thinks the idea is a good one, and she pulls the clear plastic over her now cold, pink hands.

Lift broom handle over left shoulder.
Push broom forward over wet asphalt.
Sweep dead birds into manageable piles.

Repeat.

Adjust plastic gloves.
Lift broom handle over left shoulder.
Push broom forward over wet asphalt.

When the police arrive, Colleen is fatigued and thankful for the rest. She straightens and looks at the red and blue flashing lights skimming over the corrugated building. A large van pulls up behind the police cars. Men wearing white hazardous materials suits come out of the van and hurry to the parking lot. They forbid the handling of birds. They tell everyone to stop picking up the birds and to go indoors. Colleen drops her broom to the asphalt and is about to go into the corrugated building when a small movement in a nearby pile of birds catches her attention. The olive-black wing of a robin quivers for a moment, then stops. Colleen genuflects, scoops up the robin, puts it under her cotton shirt. "It's alright, honey," she says to the belly of her shirt. "It's alright. I'll take care of you."

SWEET PEA STROLLS around the parking lot, waving her cigarette, ushering workers back to the shop floor. She tells them to stay away from the cheese. She tells them to lineup up in front of the stacks of cardboard boxes against the inside wall and to wait until someone makes a decision about what to do with the remainder of the workday. Truck drivers ignore her. They remain rooted, their hard-lined faces reddened by the chill and transfixed by flashing lights, piles of dead birds and the confusion of roving hazmat suits.

Colleen musters her courage. With cupped palms, she cradles the slight bulge under her shirt and frantically hurries into the building. The thick hotness of the room surprises her. Then she remembers the ovens cranking away despite the absence of cheese and plastic wrap. She feels safe in the familiar surroundings. Outside, the numbing chill had made her dull-headed, but now her mind is clear, her focus singular. The little one swaddled within the folds of her shirt is her only concern as she goes across the shop floor and heads briskly down an empty hallway. She pushes past a plate glass door, enters the lunchroom. "I'll get you nice and warm," she says looking down at her belly.

The lunchroom is vacant of life and bright with florescent light. A small television on the counter next to the vending machine is on; the volume is down low. A local reporter is going on about the thousands of fallen birds. "As soon as weather permits," he says, "authorities will conduct an aerial survey to determine the parameter of the incident."

Colleen goes to the microwave, opens it, gingerly puts the bird onto a small plate inside. She hesitates before closing the door. Perhaps this isn't the thing to do, she says to herself. She reaches in and cups the bird in her hands. She is aware of a tiny ribcage beneath cold feathers. After quickly scanning the room, she moves to the sink and rests the bird on a red and yellow flowered dishtowel. The bird tips onto its side, its legs are now up close to its body. She works the faucet and makes the water tepid by moving the silver knobs back and forth. She dampens another dishtowel and touches it to the bird, moves the cloth over wing feathers, strokes the orange-red chest and white throat.

As she toils, she gives her subconscious access to the television. A Fish and Game ornithologist is in the television studio. He speculates: The incident is probably due to cold temperatures or high-altitude hail rather than disease or poisoning. The camera switches to a group of people inside the mall at the edge of town. A field reporter begins to talk. "Dead birds," he says into the microphone. "What on earth is going on here?"

People scramble toward the microphone, talking at once, a verbal wall of pseudoscience and ignorance.

> *The internal navigation systems within birds is being messed with by a movement of magnetic north towards Russia.*
>
> *Some sort of infectious bird flu has struck from Vietnam.*
>
> *Man's continued sins are finally bringing about the end of the world. Praise the Lord!*

Sweet Pea takes Colleen by surprise. Suddenly she is in the lunchroom, eating a Snickers and leaning over the robin. Sweet Pea says, "L-l-looks like this pigeon has bought the farm."

Colleen puts a dry dishtowel over the body of the bird, leaving its head and closed eyes exposed to view. Then she goes over to the television and turns up the volume. "Can you believe what's happening?" she says, in an attempt to beckon Sweet Pea away from the robin.

Sweet Pea remains where she stands, drumming her fingers on the countertop, looking at the bird.

Colleen feels desperate, her stomach flip-flops. She repeats herself. "Can you believe it?" she says. "It's really difficult to understand. Guess I don't know what to believe."

Sweet Pea turns toward Colleen. Her face is unfriendly. "I have a question for you, C-colleen. Do you want to keep your job or not?"

Colleen feels scrawny next to Sweet Pea's fast-food bulk. "Huh?"

"You heard me."

"Look, I don't want any trouble. I just want to do my work and go home." She speaks slowly. Her voice is small.

"Then I'll tell you what. Let's not fuss about. Let's just get your skinny ass back onto the shop floor and against the wall like everyone else or you're fired. Is that fair enough?"

Just then, small sounds come from the yellow beak of the bird. The high-pitched *tuk-tuk* seems to grow in volume as the two surprised women turn their attention downward. Colleen looks at the white ringed eyes. The bird's strength fills her heart with admiration.

Sweet Pea moves in closer to the countertop. Her shadow falls across the bird, the bird flinches. With a quick hand movement indicative of an experienced line worker Sweet Pea snatches up the bird.

Colleen leans forward. "Don't touch it!" she shouts.

"W-what's that you're saying?"

"I mean I wish you wouldn't."

Sweet Pea ignores the appeal and drops the bird into a circular hole in the countertop next to the sink. Then she finishes her Snickers and throws the wrapper after the bird. She says, "Lady-girl, you ought to get along or I'll c-c-cut you out like a c-cancer."

Without further words, Colleen wipes her eyes and leaves the stillness of the lunchroom. She goes out onto the shop floor and finds a place next to a knee-high stack of collapsed cardboard boxes. She stands without talking, wanting to quit. But the need for money makes her stay. In a while, Sweet Pea's voice comes over the speaker system. She tells everyone to go home, get cleaned up, put on clean clothes and then return to work for overtime. She says, "I expect everyone back here in an hour. No later or there'll be trouble. We need to get these shipments out today and it'll take all of us to get it d-d-done."

Outside, the sleet is coming down sideways. Everything is white and gray except the flashing police lights. Colleen takes off her hairnet and wipes the sleet from her face, clearing her vision. She turns away from the warehouse and as she walks slowly toward her car on the far side of the parking lot she breaths warmth into her cupped hands. Her fingers are numb and the numbness makes her think of her mother's arthritis: the swollen joints, the bent fingers, the inability to find employment and the desperate concentration it takes for her to work a lighter over the end of her cigarette.

Some Good News

AFTER A DAY OF ICY DRIZZLE, the sky cleared and evening came to Chaplin, Oregon. At the north-end of town next to the railroad crossing the mill lights came on and illuminated columns of smoke and steam rising from stacks jutting up from metal rooftops. Across town, atop a small motel, yellow bulbs pulsated around an eight-foot arrow pointing to a vacancy sign. The light filtered into Mr. Wilson's room through the drapes and lit the section of carpet where he had set a briefcase loaded with rectangular wood and linoleum flooring samples. Otherwise, the room was dark.

Mr. Wilson came into the room from the shower and switched on a pole lamp. Outside, a car with a noisy muffler pulled into the parking lot. A car door slammed shut. Mr. Wilson looked across the room as if expecting someone to knock. When no one knocked, he faced the mirror above the waist-high dresser. As he worked the towel over his body, his attention went to the bags cupping his eyes, the looseness around his jaw and his protruding belly. He shook his head; pursed his lips. Recently he had needed a kick in the ass by his boss to get him out of the office and scout around for new customers. You're a smart fellow, his boss had told him, everything will be fine—you just wait and see. But Mr. Wilson could not rid himself of a cowardliness toward being middle aged.

After tugging on socks, slacks and his best button-down shirt, Mr. Wilson went to the queen bed. He dropped two quarters into the coin box attached to the headboard, stretched out onto the daisy-patterned comforter and pulled a pillow behind his head. When the bed did not vibrate, he told himself he wouldn't waste any more money. A moment later, he rolled onto his side and dropped a few more quarters into the slot. Nothing. He gave up on the idea only after slapping the metal box a few times. Suddenly he reached over to the end table and picked up the telephone receiver. He had forgotten to let Mrs. Wilson know he had arrived safely.

Mrs. Wilson answered the call. Her voice held a tone of concern. She told Mr. Wilson that she had tried to telephone him earlier, but the line was busy. "Were you on the phone about a half hour ago?" she asked.

Mr. Wilson lay on his back. "Oh, that," he said. "Sure, I had to report in with the home office."

"Well, I've been trying to call you. Sophia has a fever and a headache and I'm worried sick over it."

"I'm sure it's nothing. You know, the flu is going around."

"Honey, I don't know. . ." Mrs. Wilson paused then said, "But look at me, I'm going on without asking about your flight? How did everything go?"

"Fine, fine. Everything here is fine. After I picked up the rent-a-car, I went over to the conference center and registered. It looks to be a good crowd this year. I'm looking forward to it."

"That's good, honey. Now, about Sophia. . . she has a very bad headache and a cough, a nagging cough, otherwise I wouldn't bother you."

"I'm sure it's nothing," Mr. Wilson repeated.

"But what if it's serious? What if it's meningitis?"

As he listened, Mr. Wilson reached behind his head with his right hand and fluffed the pillow. Then he said, "Slow down, honey, I'm not taking all this in. What do you mean meningitis? What's meningitis?"

"It has something to do with swelling around the spinal cord and could be life-threatening. One of Sophia's classmates has it and she's in the hospital and it's supposed to be contagious." Mrs. Wilson's voice began to quiver. "Do you think that's what's wrong with her? Do you think she has meningitis?"

"How do I know? You're in Des Moines and I'm here in Oregon."

"Maybe I should take her to the emergency room for a blood test or something."

Mr. Wilson spoke his mind. "Look, right now we don't need any big medical bills. I'm certain it's nothing. Sophia has gotten the flu every year for the last eleven years—ever since she was born. Sometimes she's sick more than once a year. So just relax and see how things go."

"I'm worried, really worried. I don't remember her having such a headache," said Mrs. Wilson.

"Listen," said Mr. Wilson, "everything will be perfectly fine. Just give her some Tylenol and things will be better."

"Well, can I call you if she gets worse?"

It was seven-fifteen. Mr. Wilson glanced at the door. He knew he must force the conversation to an end.

"Honey, you have to be self-reliant. You have to handle the situation the best way you know how."

After a long silence, Mr. Wilson thought she now understood his point of view so he closed the conversation, telling her that he would call in the morning to check in on things. They hung up. On the whole, he felt good with the way the conversation had gone. He reached over and put another quarter in metal box attached to the headboard. Nothing.

MR. WILSON HEARD FOOTSTEPS outside his room then someone knocked. Going slowly across the room, he straightened his slacks and smoothed the sleeves of his shirt.

He opened the door and looked out at a woman whose hair hung bleach blond and limp down her back. Her face was as white as pizza dough, and she had worked a thin layer of cosmetics over the pockmarks on both cheeks. She wore a short blue cotton dress splashed with purple paisleys and stood there with hands on hips. She looked like she'd been around the block a few times, thought Mr. Wilson. But his blood began pumping quicker, just the same as if some beauty queen paid him full attention.

The woman removed the cigarette from her lips. "Hi," she said then she doubled up and began to cough. When she regained control of her breathing, she used the back of her hand to wipe her mouth. "Sorry about that."

"No harm, no foul," said Mr. Wilson.

"I'm Jackie. I got a telephone call from a Mr. Buck."

The cold air working its way into the room smelled like sawdust from the mill. Mr. Wilson put his hands in his pockets, straightened, pushed out his chest a little. "Yes, yes," he said, "I'm Mr. Buck." He knew spending money in this manner was a foolish sin but thought it would bring temporary relief from the never-ending grind.

Jackie leaned against the doorjamb, waiting for him to let her in. "I'm sorry I'm late," she said nonchalantly, controlling the edge in her voice that had blossomed during the progression from teen run-away to erotic photo shoots to stripping at the local club to hustling convention-motelers. "Just came down from Central City," she continued, "and traffic from the highway construction was a bitch."

Behind Mr. Wilson, the telephone began to ring. It rang a few times then stopped.

"It's a little chilly out here." Jackie inched closer to the doorway. "And it's not nice to keep a girl out in the cold."

Mr. Wilson was about to say something witty but paused when the telephone started up again. He tilted his head toward the ringing and blocked Jackie's entrance into the room.

Jackie became testy. "Hey, what's going on here?" she asked.

Mr. Wilson quickly shut and locked the door. When he answered the telephone, he found Mrs. Wilson at the other end of the line.

"Hi honey," said Mrs. Wilson, "I had to call so don't get furious with me. I wanted to tell you Sophia's fever has gone down and her head doesn't hurt as much. She still has that horrible cough, but it looks as if you were right about the meningitis. All the same, this whole business has put a horrible scare in me."

Mr. Wilson told her that she could now stop carrying on like some kind of mother hen and relax. "The best thing to do is to crawl into bed and get some rest," he said.

Mrs. Wilson was hesitant to hang up. "Wait!" she said. "Don't hang up. I feel silly for asking, but can we talk for a while? I need to talk to you until I settle down a bit."

Jackie began banging on the door. "Hey," she called to Mr. Wilson, "you still have to pay the full amount whether I turn the trick or not." Her voice was calm, without inflections.

He put the receiver and Mrs. Wilson's voice under the pillow and turned his attention to the door. "Beat it!" he yelled.

"Listen, I can't go back without you paying. I don't care if you slide the money under the door. But you have to pay me or so help me God I'll have to leave and call someone." Suddenly she kicked the door and yelled, "You don't fucking want me calling anyone! Is that clear?"

Mr. Wilson hurried over to the chair next to the pole lamp, picked up his jacket, felt the inside pocket. His gut wrenched. Where had he put his wallet? He returned to the bed, plopped himself down. The mattress began vibrating. Bedsprings squeaked with the gentle motion.

While Jackie beat on the door, he put the telephone receiver to his ear. Mrs. Wilson was saying ". . . commotion. I hear some sort of commotion. What's going on? Is there a problem where you're at?"

With a sideways glance, Mr. Wilson saw his wallet on the bathroom counter next to the sink. "Just a minute, honey," he said. He went to his wallet then plodded across the room to the door. His knees wobbled. His feet felt heavy, as if he wore cement slippers. He opened the door. Jackie was gone.

Mr. Wilson looked around. The evening sky was moonless. Out on the avenue in front of the motel, vehicle lights streaked back and forth. There was nearly an accident when a man staggered through traffic from the bar across the street. Mr. Wilson recognized the man as someone he had seen earlier that afternoon at the conference registration.

Mr. Wilson went back into the room and shut the door knowing somewhere out there Jackie was making a telephone call.

"Honey?" Mrs. Wilson said patiently.

Mr. Wilson ran his tongue over his bottom lip. "Listen," he said, resuming the conversation. "I can tell how distraught you are," his voice fumbled over the words, "so I have some good news for you. I'm packing up and catching the first flight home. Okay?"

"But what about the conference? What's work going to say?"

"To hell with the conference. I can't do this anymore. . ." Mr. Wilson's voice tightened. "Honey, are you still there?" he asked.

"Yes, what is it?"

"I can't wait to hold you."

"Well, that's nice to hear," said Mrs. Wilson. "I can't wait either."

They hung up. Mr. Wilson lit a cigarette and sat at the edge of the bed, which no longer vibrated. He knew he should get up, pack his stuff, drive to the airport. Instead, he sat there smoking his cigarette and thinking about Mrs. Wilson. He realized suddenly that sometime recently she had changed her hair—made it shorter or perhaps lightened it a touch.

Corbin Gets a Look

CORBIN SITS UP ON THE SOFA and runs his hand over his freshly cropped hair. He listens past the refrigerator noise. Siren wail is coming down Palm Street, getting closer, louder. It stops in front of the apartment complex where he lives. A red-light pounds against his second story window, against his living room curtains, makes the pole lamp next to the sofa into a strange dancing shadow on the far wall. He waits a moment then gets up and moves across the red-lit room, taking care to step over the empty beer cans and dirty clothes. He unlocks the front door, opens it a crack. Down there next to the curb is an ambulance with the rear door open. Two paramedics are pulling out a gurney. They put something on top of the gurney that looks like a piece of plywood with straps. Later, Corbin finds out it's called a backboard, used to immobilize an injured person for transport. People stand on the strip of lawn next to the apartment sign, watching the paramedics hurry across the sidewalk and up the concrete path leading to the stairs. One paramedic carries the head of the gurney, the other the foot.

Corbin steps out onto the concrete walkway to get a better view of things. The walkway is cold against his feet as he moves to the wrought iron railing overlooking the front of the complex. Six doors down, Tina Hernández stands against the same railing. She wears a loose fitting, short-sleeved robe. Tina and her brother are new to Paradise Apartments. The landlady had told Corbin that they moved to Ventura all the way from the jungles of Mexico, from a city called Mérida. The landlady had said, "Just think about packing up and moving to a different country when you're in your late-twenties. Can you imagine such a thing?" Corbin had tried to imagine moving to a different country, but couldn't. The landlady continued, "And," she said, "the both of them were forced to spend some time in one of those detention centers because of some kind of screw up in their visa paperwork."

Pushing the disheveled black hair from her face, Tina leans over the iron railing. "Aquí!" she screams. "Up here! Up here!" She waves one hand above her head, making the back of her arm wobble slightly.

One of the paramedics stumbles while hurrying up the stairs, falls onto his side, drops the gurney handles. "Shit," he says, sitting on the concrete step, "My ankle just rolled. It rolled then just gave out."

Corbin hurries to the stairway, goes down the steps. Without thinking, he picks up the front of the gurney. The injured paramedic gives Corbin a quick going over. Then his face relaxes and he stands up and hobbles off to one side. "Thanks man," he says. Corbin nods to him, never thinking how silly he must look, standing there in his boxer shorts and dirty t-shirt.

PEOPLE ARE NOW UP and around, crowding the second story landing and walkway. They stand with eyes choked with sleep and they talk in hushed tones.

Tina leads the way into her place, a small one-bedroom apartment. Corbin struggles through the crowd, gurney and the paramedic in tow. Inside the apartment, the window-mounted air conditioning unit struggles against the warm August night, rattling and vibrating violently in its aluminum mounting. Moisture from the evaporator coil leaks through a small crack in the plastic panel, slowly draining onto the carpet. It reminds Corbin that the unit in his apartment is leaking from an identical crack in the plastic and that he needs to let the manager know before the wet carpet begins to smell moldy again. Recently, his unit has been on the fritz with regularity, prompting him to an unfounded suspicion that something in the outside air is somehow being sucked into the compressor and being pushed through the condensing coil and jamming up the inside blower. This thought is fleeting, flashing through his brain as the paramedic at the foot of the gurney pushes him forward. They follow Tina down a short hallway lined with framed photographs of people standing in rooms with rustic furnishings. She hurries them into the bedroom where a man is sprawled on the floor between the foot of the bed and a metal stepladder. He lays on his back with arms to his sides and legs straight and slightly open. His eyes look tense.

The paramedic with the injured ankle comes into the room and mentions that he has had a bummed ankle for years. "This ankle," he says to Corbin, "it's lousy from playing weekend hoops."

Corbin looks down at the ankle then grunts.

Tina's brown eyes become wet. "He went to change the light bulb and fell off the ladder," she says.

Everyone looks up at the ceiling light fixture—the bulb is missing.

"I see," says the paramedic with the injured ankle.

The other paramedic unshoulders a medical bag. "All right, then. What's your name, sir?" he asks.

"Francisco. My name is Francisco. My legs and arms feel numb so I do not try to stand. Mi hermana call emergency number."

"Okay, Francisco, you did the right thing," says the paramedic with the medical bag. Then he pulls a small flashlight from his front pocket, drops to one knee and shines the light into Francisco's right eye. He says, "Follow the light."

Corbin stands beside Tina. They watch as the paramedics give Francisco an examination. Francisco moves his fingers. And his toes curl in response to a metal instrument dragged down the bottom of his foot. Tina lets out a loud breath of air that smells like cigarettes and wipes her nose with the palm of her hand. She says, "It was a problem with his coughing. He start to cough very, very hard and his head become dizzy. Then he fall to the floor."

As the paramedics begin the delicate process of sliding Francisco onto the backboard and strapping him in, Tina turns to Corbin and talks in a lowered voice. She says, "We come to Ventura, California to have better work. It is very difficult to find permanent work around my old home."

Corbin stares at her full volumed lips as she talks. Her Latina charm intoxicates him. He has a strong need to keep her engaged with him. "Do you miss Mexico?" he asks.

"Our home was in a very beautiful city, Mérida," she says, "it is very clean and very beautiful!"

"It must be difficult to leave your family, your friends and such a clean city. . ."

Tina's thinly groomed eyebrows arched upward. "Yes, very, very difficult. But we come here to find better opportunity, better work."

Suddenly Corbin becomes conscious of his lack of clothes. He looks down at his skinny arms, at the scar on his left forearm—an exhaust pipe burn gotten years ago from his first day at the muffler shop. Then he looks at his boxer shorts, faded with small holes and tears from the washing machine. Tina sees the embarrassment on his face and offers Francisco's grey robe. Corbin puts it on, secures the tie belt around his middle.

"Thanks a bunch," he says.

THE PARAMEDICS WORK in quick, well-orchestrated movements. They fit Francisco with a neck brace, strap him to the backboard, cover him with a blue blanket and slide him onto the gurney. Tina slips on a pair of gold colored, high block-heeled sandals. Corbin and the paramedic with the medical bag pick up the gurney. They follow Tina through the apartment. Careful not to clip the doorjamb, they leave the air conditioned coolness and maneuver onto the walkway, into a night heavy with summer heat. Gripping the gurney handles and walking backwards, Corbin leads the way through the murmuring crowd and then down the flight of stairs. He knows the injured man he carries is an immigrant, but he doesn't know exactly what that means. He can't understand the kind of backbone necessary to move to a different country. A move like that, he thinks, isn't for people afraid of loneliness or afraid of ridicule. A move like that, he thinks, isn't for cowards. Yes, a move like that requires a set of big testicles. *Cojones grande*, he believes is the proper phrase.

When they get to the concrete pathway, the paramedic with the injured ankle helps Corbin with a lever that releases some folding legs with wheels. Then Corbin steps back and lets the paramedic with the medical bag push Francisco toward the ambulance. As the paramedics slide the gurney into the rear compartment, Tina folds her arms beneath her breasts and looks up and down the neighborhood. City glow brushes over the night sky, concealing the stars. Plenty of people are milling around. Others are straggling back to their kitchens. It had become a good opportunity for cooking a late-night snack.

She says, "I love Ventura. The hospital here will soon make Francisco well."

Corbin scratches his burn scar, as he often did when nervous. "Yeah," he says. "Everything will be copasetic. You'll see."

Tina lights a cigarette, waves it around. Emotion chokes her voice. "Y-yes, I must not be estupid. Things will turn out fine and good." Suddenly she steps in close to Corbin. Streetlamp glow smooths her face, glosses over worry-lines and tear streaks. "Can I ask your name?" she says.

"Cole Corbin. Friends call me Corbin."

"I'm Tina. Your favor, Corbin, I very much like. Now we are no more strangers. You live here in apartments?"

"Sure, I'm over there in #215."

"Okay. I see you before, but you wear long hair before. Yes?"

"Sure. Had me some plans to enlist so I recently got a high and tight." Corbin runs his hand over the bristles covering his scalp then he continues. "But maybe I have a change of mind about enlisting. Maybe I'm staying here."

"Yes, I think that would be a nice thing," she says.

Suddenly she stands on her tiptoes and grips Corbin's shoulders. Her hands are shaking as she hugs him. He inhales her smoky breath. The thin hairs on the back of his hands twitch. He senses he should return the gesture. But he hesitates and then the moment is over, his chance gone. Tina flips her cigarette to the ground, climbs wearily into the back of the ambulance and plops down on an aluminum bench across from her brother, secure for transport. She gives Corbin a look that embodies concern for her brother's health and frustration about missing her cousin's recent wedding in Mérida and anger over her detainment when crossing the San Ysidro Port of Entry between San Diego and Tijuana and a longing for Mama's homemade panuchos. Nobody prepares pulled pork like Mama. Corbin noticed this look and is sure it's a solicitation for him to ask her out when things settle down. Damn straight, he thinks.

The paramedics shake Corbin's hand then go away. Siren wail dirties the neighborhood. The ambulance races down Palm Street, past the liquor store and fairground, toward Community Memorial Hospital. When the flashing lights fade from view,

Corbin just stands there on the sidewalk, scratching his burn scar, thinking. He sees himself inside the ambulance, strapped tightly to the gurney. The two-way radio is going. He is conscious of the dispatch communications coming to him in a continuous string of incomprehensible voices and static. And the surrounding walls with its shelves of diagnostic equipment and medication makes him feel as if he is in some kind of laboratory. Tina is there, sitting on a long bench. She looks worried. When she bends over to kiss him, her long hair falls across his chest and her robe unfolds.

Corbin stands there until the clouded look covering his face goes away. As he turns from the street and moves through the remaining rubberneckers, he tightens Francisco's robe about himself. Now he becomes aware of the neighborhood smells: a late-night burger on a fry pan, tortillas in the microwave, spilled beer, tobacco and reefer smoke. And an eerie feeling comes to him, as if he is suddenly walking through a carnival or county fair or traveling circus.

The Accident

THREE DAYS AFTER NEWS of his father's death, Mike pulled his pickup into the Phillips 66 filling station on the outskirts of Salford, Nebraska. The early evening air was humid. Sweat beaded Mike's forehead as he replaced the pump nozzle into its cradle and secured the gas cap into place. After scraping and washing the windshield of bug splatter from the fifteen-hour drive from Birmingham and using the toilet facility, he went into the convenience store. Inside, the air was thick with instrumental arrangements of popular country songs and the smells of body order, bleach, coffee and hotdogs turning on the roller grill. Mike grabbed a box of Oreos and a twenty-ounce bottle of water.

The man at the register behind the checkout counter went to the same high school that Mike went to—fifteen years ago.

"Hey, Paul, you're looking fit," Mike lied. Paul had been a stalwart boy in high school. He had been able to throw a twelve-pound iron ball sixty feet down field at nearly every meet. Now he was overweight and soft.

Paul stood there, scrutinizing the person in front of him: even tan, sandy hair curling over his ears, baggy orange shorts, pineapple print button shirt, white slip-on deck shoes. Paul looked for a long moment then he smiled. "Mike Lockhart? Is that you?"

"Yep, it's me."

"Damn, you're the one looking fit. What have you been doing to get them arms?"

"Spent the last fifteen years working on a charter fishing vessel. Keeps me hopping."

"I heard something about that. Nothing beats getting paid for exercising, huh? Shit, now a-days my exercise involves getting the tongs, clamping one of them hot dogs and slapping it in a white bread bun."

They laughed.

Paul said, "Let me guess, you've had enough a Florida, and you're moving back to paradise?"

Mike explained about the telephone call that he had received three days past. It had been the Salford Community Hospital. The woman had been a fast talker. "Is this Mike Lockhart?" "Yes." "Is your father Nolan Lockhart, age sixty-four, of 572 N. Butter Cloud Avenue?" "Yes." "Well, sir, I'm sorry to inform you," she had said, "that he died last night. Heart attack. I'm sorry." Then she asked if he could come to the hospital to arrange for the body to be collected by a funeral home. There was also his personal belongings to be dealt with. After a long silence, she added that they would be more than happy to help with the proper forms to get a death certificate.

"So there you have it," Mike said. "Pops dead at 64."

"Damn," Paul broke in, "I'm sorry to hear this."

"Thanks."

"You never know when your number is up, huh?"

"Ain't that the truth." Mike reached over with his right hand, rubbed his left shoulder. It had been a long two days. First, there had been the seven-hundred-mile trip from Cape Coral, where he lived, to Birmingham, where he was met by a lousy Motel 6 mattress. Then another nine hundred to get to Salford. Road vibrations. Bad posture on the drive. Shoulders and neck aching. Foot cramping.

"Hey, you think you'll give Jenny a call?" Paul asked.

"Nope. Figured she's married with a couple teens by now."

"She's not."

"Not what?"

"All of the above."

"Huh. . ."

"So you calling her?"

"Don't know. Not sure this is the best time for a reunion. Kind of got a lot on my plate."

"You got to seize the day, man. Don't be some kind of dumb bastard, you hear me? You got to seize the day." It was something Paul had chanted before each high school track meet: *You got to seize the day. . .* he had said over and over. "Hey," he continued, "you want to get a hot dog for the road?"

Mike declined the offer and told Paul it was great to see him and that he should take care. Then he scooped up his change, grabbed the plastic grocery bag and headed toward the plate glass door. Once outside, he hurried over the oil-stained asphalt to his pickup. As he buckled his seat belt, he became conscious of Jennifer's close proximity. It had been an agonizing drive, his thoughts constantly bouncing back and forth between Pops and her. He didn't know what to do about Jennifer. His mind was jammed with indecision. Exasperated, he tore open the box of Oreos and stuffed two into his mouth before starting the motor.

Before heading to Pops's, he took a detour down Sixth. The sun was low. Most of the buildings and neighborhoods were in shadow. He drove past the Dairy Queen and pulled over in front of his old house. It was a two bedroom/one bath affair with a carport attached to the south side of the house. He had spent from the ages of eight until eighteen in that corner bedroom. Before that, he lived in Lincoln. Then after high school he left everything, moved to Florida. He remembered the day before leaving town, he and Jennifer in that corner room, sunshine filtering in through threadbare curtains making the sweat in her hair glint like welding splatter.

From Sixth, Pops's place was only a few minutes away. As Mike made his way down Ninth, his mind was still jammed with indecision. The small houses painted yellow and blue and white with rooftop satellite dishes and cyclone fences around front yards cluttered with plastic pools and huge oak trees went unnoticed. He turned onto Butter Cloud. Mid-block he slowed and parked in front of the red bricked, white steepled First Christian Fellowship building. Across the street was the three-story Victorian where Pops had rented a room for the past fifteen years.

MIKE GOT OUT OF HIS PICKUP, flipped his cigarette to the ground and grabbed his duffle and plastic grocery bag from the passenger seat. Skeeters buzzed around him, one landed on his neck and bit him before he could brush it away. Some chickens hurried past his pickup, moved to a patch of dirt under an oak and began noisily scratching the earth. He crossed the street, made his way to the side of the Victorian rooming house. Exhausted, he went up the external wooden steps to the second floor landing and stepped into a short hallway dimly lit by a single overhead light. There were two room doors on each side of the hallway. In front of the second door on the right sat a woman. A grocery bag leaned against her folded legs. Upon seeing Mike, she stood up. They stared at one another for a moment before she came over. She wore cutoff Levi's shorts and a thin red tank top with a white heart and white lettering stenciled on the front: HUSKERS GIRL. Blue butterfly hair clips kept her straw-color bangs from her eyes. He dropped his bags to the dirty carpet, and she wrapped her arms around him. He closed his eyes and pulled her body close to his, letting himself enjoy her warmth.

"It's good to see you Jenn," he whispered.

"I'm sorry to hear about Pops," she said.

"Thanks."

Her voice was nice to hear. There was no awkwardness as they broke apart. *Some people are like that, time between visits doesn't bring self-consciousness. There is always a natural comfort.* He gave her a questioning look.

"Paul gave me a call, said you stopped by the station, told me what was going on."

"He was like that in high school, always blabbing about something that wasn't his business. But, yeah, this time I'm glad he blabbed."

Then she said, "So Mikey, love the outfit. Orange shorts. Pineapple shirt. Current fashion in Florida?"

"Pretty much. You know, when in Rome. . ."

Mike unlocked the door with a key Pops had sent him two years ago. Jennifer leaned into him as he opened the door. She smelled fresh: gardenias and citrus. A perfume she wore in high school, he remembered. He flipped a wall switch, and a ceiling light went on. The room was small. There were no wall hangings or decorations or photographs. A window took up most of the street-side wall. Pushed up close to the left-side wall was a single bed without a headboard. There was no built-in closet, just a small armoire and a long dresser on the right-side wall. Both looked like third or fourth-hand furniture. On the dresser top was a bottle of water, a bottle of Pepto-Bismol, a rectangular seven-day pill organizer, a pack of Chesterfields and Pops's work gloves for his warehouse and loading dock job at the All Season's Nursery.

Mike set his duffle and grocery bag on the floor and looked at the paper Safeway sack in Jennifer's arms.

"What's all that about?"

"Two sandwiches: turkey/Swiss for me; ham/pepper jack for you. You still like pepper jack don't you?"

"Yep, still my favorite cheese."

"Good. I also got a container of potato salad and two Silver Bullets. You still like Silver Bullets, don't you?"

"Yep, still my favorite beer. So how'd you have time to buy all this stuff?"

"I'm fast when it's important."

"And this is important?"

"This is most important."

Mike stomped his left foot on the floor. "These damn cramps," he explained. "It's been a helluva drive and my body's feeling it."

Jennifer set the grocery bag next to his duffle. "When did you find out?" she asked.

His eyes glazed. His face mirrored the sadness he felt in his heart. "Early Wednesday morning," he said. "And the next day I was off, heading here." He told her about stopping in Birmingham and about the lousy mattress and his lack of sleep and his continuous foot cramp and all the windshield bugs as he drove through the croplands lining the highway. Flatlands covered with tall wheat and corn waiting for the fall harvest. Flatlands. And bugs.

Mike glanced around the room.

Jennifer said, "Guess he liked bare walls."

"There used to be stuff," he said. "Look up close."

Jennifer went up to the wall, gave it a good look. "There's a bunch of little nail holes in the plaster."

"Two years ago, he had a ministroke. Seems he felt better after a few days and there wasn't any permanent damage. But I think it shook him up because shortly afterwards he sent me a box crammed with old school papers and photos. Some of the photos were framed, like he'd took them from the wall and tossed them into the box. Even Riley's stuff was there. She was six at the time of the accident, so there wasn't much that belonged to her." He sighed. "Shit," he said.

"What?"

"Just thinking."

Jennifer changed the subject. "How about us going outside and getting some air. You up for a twenty-minute walk before sandwich-supper?"

"How do you know I didn't eat something on the road?"

"Paul said you looked hungry and only bought a box of Oreos."

"Again with Paul. You know, he was trying to sell me a hot dog. I think he gets commission for selling hot dogs."

Jennifer picked up the Safeway bag. Mike took it from her. "I can carry this," he said.

AS THEY WENT DOWN the narrow steps Jennifer told Mike she knew the perfect place for a picnic. But she would not let on where it was. Mike stopped at the bottom of the staircase, lit two cigarettes.

"Thanks." She took a moment to inhale the cigarette smoke then she led the way around the Victorian, through the backyard and up to the railroad tracks that ran parallel to Butter Cloud.

Mike's eye followed her movements. She was still eye-catching. *I'm glad she's here.*

He said, "I still think about you, you know."

Her whole face smiled. "Really?"

"Yeah, really."

She said, "So I hear you've been working on some fishing boat."

Mike gave her a look.

"Yeah," she laughed, "Paul again."

"I'm first mate for a charter fishing operation. Where I live is big for recreational fishing, big for catching tarpon." He told her that he worked on a boat that ran out of Salty Sam's Marina in Fort Meyers. "We take our customers to waters around

Sanibel Island and Captiva Island," he said, "show them a good time."

She stepped onto one of the hot rolled steel railroad rails and used her arms for balance as she walked.

"So, Jenn, what are you doing these days?" he asked.

She looked at him over her shoulder and in doing so lost her balance. Quickly she was back at it, moving along the rail. "Working over at Sunrise Café."

"Sunrise. That was one of our favorites."

"They still got great food. And before that, I worked as a bookkeeper for Jay's Janitorial Services. Did that for over five years then went to Sunrise. The money's better when you include tips."

It was close to nine o'clock. Distant sunglow edged the low sprawling Nebraska foothills. They had left the houses behind and were now in an area where vacant fields flanked the road that ran parallel to the tracks. A short distance ahead was the Farmer's CO-OP with its silo and grain elevator. When they came to the silo Jennifer hopped off the rail, grabbed Mike's hand and led him across the road to an abandoned diner. Although its windows and doors were boarded up, a group of picnic tables remained chained to the concrete outdoor dining area.

Mike said, "Hey, I remember this place. We used to go here for birthday celebrations when we were kids."

They sat down. Mike placed the bag on the table and opened the two Silver Bullets. Then he lit a cigarette and transferred it to her outstretched fingers. As he lit one for himself, Jennifer explained that the owners had retired six years ago and no one bought the business. No one wanted it.

"I loved their burgers," he said after a swallow of beer. "You know, I hardly recognized things as I drove through town this afternoon. I feel like an outsider now. And this place. . . I remember you and I were kids here, cramming our faces with fries and ice cream. And now what? I'll tell you what. Now we're thirty-three. How did that happen?"

When did all this growing up happen? How. . . how did Pops get so old?

The sun disappeared. Dusk set in. Suddenly security and working lights illuminated the silo and grain elevator in sheets of blue and white. Jennifer handed Mike his sandwich. They became silent. As they ate, it became darker. Cicadas jammed the twilight with their chirp-like buzzing. The humid air coaxed from the surrounding dirt an ammonia-like smell due to the dirt's lack of oxygen and proper drainage.

"You know," he said, pointing to a boarded-up window. "I remember looking out that window with Pops and seeing those lights come on. I told him it looked like some kind of spaceship."

"What'd he say?"

"Nothing. He said nothing. You know, I was never able to figure that guy out. He was supportive but distant at the same time. Maybe it was somehow my fault."

Jennifer said, "It wasn't you." She sat between him and the grain elevator, her body outlined by the lights. She continued, "He was like that with everyone. My parents thought he never got over what happened to your sister."

"I wish I could remember her. Everything about her is a mystery. Even her name is strange on my tongue. *Riley*. The only thing I know about her is that she was hit and killed by a car when we lived in Lincoln, when I was eight. She was in the front yard by herself messing around with one of those red rubber balls. Pops was supposed to be watching her, but he was doing something else. I'm told she ran into the street after the ball. A short while after the accident Mom moved out, just picked up and left. And that was that."

"I wonder why she left."

"So do I."

She blamed him, that's why! Pops screwed up. If it wasn't for him, Riley's story wouldn't have ended so soon. He should have kept an eye on her. He screwed up!

Across the street a large grain truck came into view and parked next to the two-hundred-foot wooden elevator. Loose feed grain spilled down the chute into the truck bed. Grain dust clouded up against the flood of electric light. The truck's driver side window was down and Mike could hear radio music. It was a familiar song. A song played at his Senior Ball.

He remembered the dance. "Oh, I love this song," Jennifer had said of the same song now playing from the truck. He remembered her singing. With her arms raised above her head, she had danced slow circles over the gymnasium floorboards. He had stood there silently watching her until she cozied up to him. He put his calloused hand on the small of her back. Her paisley-printed, figure-hugging sundress was wet with sweat. The floor was crowded, the music loud, but he heard her clearly. "Do I make you happy?" "You're a midnight ride under a harvest moon," he had told her, attempting to soften what he needed to say. And then he said, "Look Jenn, I have to tell you something." "Huh?" "I said I need to tell you something." "Well go ahead." "Let's go outside where we have some privacy." Outside, she leaned against the gymnasium wall under the gooseneck light. He told her that after graduation he planned to move to Florida. "Come with me," he had said. "I can't," she told him. A whippoorwill had been singing nearby. He remembered focusing on the whippoorwill's song, trying to shut out her sobbing.

Mike shoved his sandwich wrapper and crushed potato salad container into the grocery bag. He said, "I'm supposed to go to the hospital tomorrow at 1:30. First floor reception. Supposed to ask for someone named Cassidy." He suddenly had a notion of Pops at the hospital, waiting for his son, sheet covered body lying in some long drawer. "You know, Jenn, this whole thing is freaking me out."

Suddenly Jennifer blurted: "I should have gone to Florida with you when you asked."

Mike gathered her right hand into both of his hands. "I hated to leave you."

"I admired you after you left. If you hadn't cut out of town so fast, I would have probably changed my mind and tagged along."

He admitted his departure was abrupt. Looking back, it was all a whirlwind in his mind. *Pops had had stent surgery a few months before the Senior Ball. Afterwards he started going on and on about how I needed to get away, start something for myself.* Mike said, "Pops was the one who gave me the contact in Florida. He gave me the Stoll's address. Said it was a couple he knew when we lived in Lincoln. Captain Stoll owns the boat I work on. His wife teaches fourth grade. They set me up in their backyard bungalow." He went on to tell her that they did not have kids and that they sort of adopted him, in a semi-strange way.

Mike could see her turning the story around in her mind. Finally, she said, "I admired your freedom. I should have gone with you but I was afraid."

"Of what?"

"Everything. I was afraid to choose between staying with my parents and going with you. Afraid to test new waters. Afraid of living without a safety net." Her face sagged with unhappiness. She continued, "How come we never wrote to each other? And after the first few telephone conversations, how come we didn't call each other anymore?"

They sat for a while exchanging glances without saying anything.

"God, this is awkward. I'm sorry," she murmured.

There was a moment of tenseness then Mike leaned into her, used his forefinger to wipe the perspiration from her left cheek. She let him kiss her lips. Surrounded by the twilight, they kissed hard. Her smell made him lightheaded. He slid his forefinger under her right tank top strap and made little caressing circles upon her collarbone then he untwist the thin shoulder strap of her tank top, damp and clingy from humidity.

How many years has it been since I felt her kiss? Over fifteen. Damn, how did I let that happen? Why did I let that happen? What's wrong with me?

Mike stood up "I should be getting back to Pops's place," he said. "I'd like to pack up a few of his things before I get too tired."

ON THE WAY BACK to Pops's the twilight faded into darkness. The white-gray crushed rock beneath the tracks was now scarcely visible. If it was not for the strong smoky scent of creosote coming from the railroad ties, Mike and Jennifer would be unaware of the railroad tracks just a few feet away. They walked hand in hand and laughed when the other stumbled into some pothole or tripped over scattered railroad spikes that littered the path.

Gradually residential lights came into view. And as they hurried past backyards, they were keenly aware of the blueish glow of televisions behind curtained windows. When they reached the Victorian they circled to the front, to Butter Cloud, and retrieved a stack of collapsed cardboard boxes from the bed of Mike's pickup.

Mike spoke as they made their way up the steps. "I think I'm going to spend some time tonight to take stock of things," he said. At the second-floor landing, he stopped and told Jennifer that before heading to the hospital tomorrow he intended to run Pops's belongings over to the Goodwill. Suddenly a thought came to him. He said, "I've also got to buy a shredder to take care of Pops's bills and medical records. Damn, tomorrow's going to be a busy day."

They entered the room and flipped on the overhead light. Music was streaming through the wall from the neighboring room. Jenn snuggled up to him and he put his arms around her slender waist. For a moment, he let himself feel her warmth, let his fingertips touch the small of her back.

"You know," he said, "after I left home Pops and I drifted apart. He didn't want me visiting."

"How come?"

"I think he was embarrassed about his living situation, the fact that he didn't have a bed for me, that I would have had to sleep on the floor. Yeah right, like sleeping on the floor would bother me. And I couldn't get him to visit me. Not sure why that was. I offered to pick up his plane fare and all, but he adamantly refused." Mike told her that the Stoll's have plenty of rooms, plenty of space to accommodate a visitor, plenty of space to accommodate Pops and his privacy.

Jennifer didn't know what to say. She changed the subject. "When do you have to get back to Florida?" she asked.

"I got a couple days here then I've got to get back."

"Is there a chance you'd stay longer? Maybe you could stay for the 4th of July Parade."

"Jenn, I can't. But I have to say, it was cool watching the Co-Op lights go on. Seeing them was a great idea. A great treat. Thanks."

"That's no substitute for our world-famous 4th of July Parades."

"World famous?"

"Okay, so not world famous. But what about our December snow. Don't you miss that? And what about our meaty chili and sweet cinnamon rolls?"

"Well, now I have other things like fresh fish." He grinned.

"Thick steaks."

"Beaches. And I'm a boat ride away from a bunch of cool islands and keys: Sanibel, Captiva, Lovers Key. And we have dolphins. Who doesn't love dolphins?"

"Don't you think that maybe you're back where you belong?"

"Jenn, my roots are now deep in Florida. I'm at home in my situation. In Florida I have a good future."

He felt her body slacken against his. "To be honest," she said, "all that sounds nice. I'm happy for you."

He broke away, moved across the room to the dresser. "I hate to say this, but I got to get started on this Pops stuff before I fall asleep." He looked at her. She was smiling. Suddenly it struck him that before a few hours ago it had been over fifteen years since seeing her. "You don't need to stay if you don't want," he said.

"Pshh. . . What do you want me to do?" she said.

"I'll take the dresser. You take the armoire. Remove the clothes and stack them near the bed. Tomorrow I'll go through everything and figure out what's right for the Goodwill."

THE ARMOIRE was double-doored. Half the unit was fitted with a coat rod, the other half was fitted with four drawers. As Jennifer went to work removing jackets and long-sleeved shirts from metal hangers, Mike started in with the dresser. They worked in silence, half listening to the muffled music coming through the wall. The first drawer Mike opened was crammed with socks, underwear and pill containers. He placed the clothes on the floor at the end of the dresser and left the containers in the drawer. Four pairs of blue jeans were in the next drawer. These he stacked next to the piles Jennifer had created.

"Huh," he said as he opened the next drawer.

"What?"

Mike stared down at a drawer cluttered with large manila envelopes.

"I don't know. There seems to be a bunch of paperwork in here."

Jennifer said, "Well, check it out."

There were five envelopes, the contents of each were labeled in black marker across the front.

He retrieved the first three.

Savings & Checking
Investments
Life Insurance

The contents made the envelopes bulge. *I can't think about money or inheritance at this point.* He placed the material on top of the dresser. The next envelope was labeled:

Funeral Arrangements.

"Looks like he's already made some plans for his burial," he said.

"What does he want?"

"A while ago he told me he wanted to be cremated. I'm sure it's all here in this envelope, but I'm not ready to open it."

Jennifer turned and faced him. "That's okay," she said. "Don't feel rushed. You can do it tomorrow before going to the hospital."

He added the envelope to the stack, and then placed *Medical Records* on top of it.

The last envelope, the envelope still at the bottom of the drawer, made his body surge with adrenaline. He became lightheaded as he stared down at the black marker word *Riley*. "What's this?" he uttered. And as he looked at his dead sister's name, he somehow knew that the contents of the envelope would change the way he looked at things, the way he understood his past. It was one of those unfounded feelings people sometimes have.

He retrieved the envelope and was about to open it when he decided to go across the room and sit down upon the bed. Jennifer came over, sat beside him, hugged her knees to her chest. She kept silent as he opened the seal flap and withdrew a two-page emergency room report from a hospital in Lincoln. Mike's eyes went to the highlighted box summarizing Riley's ER check-in and her ensuing death.

Patient Name: Riley Isabel Lockhart

Age: Six years

Symptoms: Loss of consciousness, seizures, pupil dilation, clear fluid drainage from nose and ears.

Diagnosis: Traumatic head injury

Cause of Death: Severe skull fracture hematoma resulting from blunt force trauma to the head from brick projectile.

A brick? Mike's eyes teared. Jennifer was talking but to him it was just muffled noise. A brick? Blunt force trauma? Suddenly it came to him that he had no idea how his sister had died. At that moment, his past detached itself from his accepted version of reality and left him with a hole. He stood up and began talking rapidly. "What does this mean? Who the hell can I talk to in order to get to the bottom of this?" He was now shouting. All his life he believed his father had been negligent in keeping an eye on her as she played with some ball in the front yard. He believed his sister was killed after being struck by a car, not by some brick. "This doesn't make any sense! This doesn't make any fucking sense!"

The music in the next room suddenly stopped, leaving Mike and Jennifer in silence. Pops's room seemed to close in on him.

Mike said, "I need a minute to pull myself together, to calm down." He grabbed Pops's pack of Chesterfields from the dresser, went into the hallway and lit a cigarette. His heart pounded hard as he paced the hallway. *Why after all these years was this happening to me? Why was it happening now, as if Pops's death wasn't hard enough to stomach? What have I done to deserve all of this?* He finished his cigarette, lit another. When he returned to the room, Jennifer was slipping her phone into the back pocket of her cutoffs.

"I called her," she said.

"Called who?"

"Lori Kohl, that's who."

Jennifer told him about the name and telephone number of a family contact at the bottom of the hospital report. "Someone named Lori Kohl," she said, "so I called her. She talked to me as if she had been expecting the call. She knows you. . . I mean she knew you when you were a kid in Lincoln. She gave me her address and directions. She's expecting us to swing by tomorrow morning."

"Wait a minute, what are you talking about?"

"Apparently, this woman saw everything. But she doesn't want to talk over the phone about it. She wants us to go to her house in the morning. She said nineish would be a good time for her."

"You're shitting me?"

"Mikey, I shit you not. We can swing by in the morning and make it back here in time for your hospital appointment."

"What do you mean *we* can swing by?"

"I'm going with you. I've already called work and took the day off."

"Jenn, you don't have to do this."

"The hell you say."

Mike apologized for losing his temper. She told him that she would have done the same. Then she asked if she could stay the night. "I'll stay here if you don't mind," she said. "That way we can get an early start." The ash was long on his cigarette. He motioned with it. "You can take the bed," he said. "I'll take the floor."

Jennifer closed the distance between them. They hugged. "Thank you," he whispered. "Let's get some shut eye," she said. Then she went over to the bed, pulled the blanket up over the dirty sheets and lay down on her back. Mike went to the window, grabbed a hold of the grimy sill and pushed it open for some fresh air.

MIKE SUFFERED through a mostly sleepless night. When he did sleep, he found himself dreaming of dark heavy-looking cumulonimbus clouds from which fell an unceasing stream of rectangular bricks. The bricks caused extensive property damage and loss of life. In the center of the devastation lay Riley's corpse. Her expressionless little girl face lacked color. Her head was a cracked melon.

The next morning the smell of wet earth came into the room. From his spot on the floor, Mike could see out the window. A light summer drizzle fell from a putty gray sky. He sat up, stretched his arms above his head, twisted his torso from side to side. Every muscle was stiff and ached.

The ceiling light was still on, bathing everything in a dingy yellowish color. Jennifer was sound asleep. Mike went downstairs to the kitchen and found a jar of Folgers and a mug. He worked the microwave to heat some water and coffee crystals. Returning to the window in Pops's room, he stood sipping coffee, letting his eyes wander, letting his mind wander. The graveled walkway connecting the front and back yards was wet, riddled with shallow puddles. Soon the rain ran its course and the clouds moved along, leaving a reddish-yellow morning light.

Finishing his coffee, he returned downstairs, made a cup for Jennifer. Seeing Jenifer wake up made him feel better. She appreciated the coffee, and as they ravaged the box of Oreos they discussed the day ahead. Mike was at a loss as to the identity of Lori Kohl. He felt he should know of her, but his mind would not give up even an inkling. Before they left for Lincoln, Jennifer grabbed the envelope, the one marked funeral arrangements, and put it in her oversized purse.

Outside a slight breeze had kicked in, bringing with it the sweet smell of wet earth. Birds came down to the graveled walkway from a nearby oak and enjoyed themselves in the puddles. Everything was wet. In need of some traction tape, the stairs were slippery. Mike and Jennifer used the stair railing to keep safe. When they reached the bottom step Mike lit a cigarette for each of them. They got into his pickup and he ran the wipers for a few swipes to clear the rain-wet windshield. Then he headed toward Highway 34. As he merged onto the highway his excess speed caused his truck's tires to hydroplane. "Christ, Mikey, slow down a bit," she said. He ignored her comment. As he drove, a painful sadness hung on him. After a while, Jennifer offered to open the envelope. "It probably has information you'll need for the hospital people," she said. He supposed she was right.

Jennifer opened the envelope and inspected its contents. As he drove, Mike glanced at the top of the page: SWEENEY & SONS FUNERAL CARE.

Jennifer said, "He's already paid for cremation, even picked an urn"

Mike told her that Pops had mentioned cremation several times during their phone calls over the years. He said, "Over the past few days I've been thinking about this. I've decided to take him to Florida, give him a burial at sea. I've done it before. Burials at sea. People have hired us to take their loved ones to a good spot to scatter the ashes. I just never figured I'd be doing it for Pops. It's always an event. Big groups show up. You know, cousins and the like. Family members. But for Pops I guess it will be just me."

Jennifer said, "Can I come? I'd like to join you."

"You mean come to Florida?"

"Yeah. Maybe even stay if you want me too."

Mike's vision darted back and forth from the road to her.

She told him that although she was a Huskers Girl at heart, she would be willing to change. She said, "I like beaches too. And fresh fish sounds good to me."

"You know, you can still get a good steak in Florida. It's not all seafood."

After an awkward moment, she said, "There's no one special waiting for you back there?"

"No. There's no one, only the couple I rent the bungalow from."

"So you didn't answer my question. Do you want me to go with you and stay?"

He sat, quietly, trying to come up with the right words.

She said, "Mikey, tell me what you want."

Don't be a goddamn fool. Listen to the hotdog pusher. Seize the day.

He stumbled over the words. "I'd be lying if I said I didn't want you to come along."

"Do you think you could love me again?"

"I never stopped loving you," he said.

She put her hand on his leg.

He could feel her hand trembling.

She said, "In Florida, *I* wouldn't have to wear one of those pineapple shirts, would I?"

"Naw." he said, "For you, I recommend the flamingos and tropical leaves pattern."

"The hell you say," she chuckled.

He took his right hand off the wheel and rested it on top of hers.

AFTER SEVERAL WRONG TURNS, they found their way to a quiet middle-class neighborhood. Big puffy clouds floated across a rain-scrubbed field of blue. Mike parked his pickup in front of a beige split-level house with green shutters. A 4th of July inspired wreath hung from the front door: red, white, blue, with a corrugated tin sign in the center–*America The Beautiful.*

As they moved up the walkway Jennifer reached over, took hold of Mike's hand. The door opened before they got to the front step and an older woman positioned herself in the frame. "Michael, is that you?"

"Yes, it's me. . ." he said.

"What a handsome man you've become."

"Thank you, ma'am." *Who is this woman, this Lori Kohl? How does she fit into this monkey show?*

Mrs. Kohl was a short woman, chest-level to Mike. She wore her hair short and reddish orange. Her weight was under control, maybe a few extra pounds in the arms and waist. A set of two-pound weights were velcroed around her ankles. She ushered Mike and Jennifer into the entryway. "Come in," she said amiably. "Come on in." The house smelled sweet and pleasant, like bakery air.

Mike said, "Thank you for seeing us. But I have to say I don't remember you. I don't remember anything about living in Lincoln for that matter. It's all fuzzy in my mind."

"I'd be surprised if you did." She turned and led them from the entryway to the breakfast nook. "You can sit here," she pointed to a corner coffee shop-like booth. They slid in. There was an urn of coffee on a mat in the middle of the table. Mrs. Kohl poured three cups and slid in next to Jennifer. Jennifer said. "You have a nice house, Mrs. Kohl." Mrs. Kohl smiled and leaned forward to get a better view of Mike. "Your parents," she said, "moved here after getting jobs with the school district. A year later you were born. You left when you were eight."

"School district?"

"Your parents were teachers. I'm guessing you didn't know that."

"Teacher? Pops a teacher?"

"Both your parents taught."

"Both?"

"Your father taught sixth grade. Your mother first."

"Sixth grade? I don't believe it. Pops wasn't a children-type-of-person."

"He quit because being around all those kids reminded him of Riley."

My mind can't handle all this jumbling!

Mrs. Kohl put her cup down and pointed across the street. "That's your old house."

Mike and Jennifer stood up and looked out the window at the house on the other side of the street. It was difficult for him to believe he was looking at the house he lived in up until the age of eight. It all looked strange, nothing familiar. There was a brick planter along the walkway. *I sort of remember that brick planter.*

Mrs. Kohl got up, went to the countertop between oven and sink then returned with a homemade loaf of bacon walnut bread, some honey butter and three 4th of July themed cloth napkins. As she walked, she made an effort to lift her knees high, making the most of her ankle weights.

Mike and Jennifer took advantage of her baking, each grabbing a large slice.

"This is the window I was looking out when I saw it happen." Mrs. Kohl spoke as if she was in some sort of trance, as if she was some kind of spiritual medium tuning into Mike's history. "I was looking out the window and I saw it all. When it happened, Riley, your little sister, was sitting in the middle of the driveway, swinging her little net, trying to catch the butterflies flitting around her. Lord, I still dream about it, still wake up in the middle of the night and cry. Your father was building that brick planter out in front. He loved flowers, the different colors, the different fragrances. The day before the accident, he had stacked the bricks on the lawn at the edge of the driveway. Well, there you and Scotty were, fooling around as boys do."

Mike interrupted, "Who's Scotty?"

"Scotty was my boy, God rest his soul. Anyway, you two were taking bricks and tossing them across the lawn area, seeing who could throw the furthest. Up until that point an overhand throw seemed to fit you both. But Scotty couldn't match the distance you were making. Well, my boy grabbed a brick and did something different. He threw it underhanded. Only he released the brick too late. It went backwards, arching over the brick pile and landing on top of Riley's head." Mrs. Kohl touched her own head, the crown portion.

Mike's eyes widened. "What?"

"The brick went backwards," she repeated, "hitting her in the head. Right here." Again, Mrs. Kohl touched the spot.

Tears ran from Jennifer's eyes.

Mike stood up, looked at the planter across the street. Suddenly a strange thought occurred to him. "Do you mean to tell me that one of those bricks might be the one that killed my sister?"

"Good Heaven's no. After the police came and looked at the brick, your father pounded it with a hammer. Then he swept up the dust and dumped it all in the garbage."

"Why wasn't Pops watching us, keeping an eye on things?"

"Your father was at the nursery getting flowers for that planter. Your mother was the one supervising you kids."

"My mother? What the hell. . ."

Mrs. Kohl was an articulate woman with a panache for the dramatic. She used her hands and arms as she explained herself, waving them this way and that. Yes, Mike's mother should have been watching the kids. After the accident, she took on all the blame. She became inconsolable. Living normal day-to-day activities became impossible for her. Finally, she left. It was then that the fabrications began. The rubber ball story, for one. "And the bit about him watching you kids during play," she said.

"I don't get it. Why would he take the blame?"

"Well, at the time he didn't want you knowing your mother was responsible for the lack of supervision. He didn't want you blaming her, hating her. He had this crazy notion she would eventually come home. He wanted it to be easy for her to return."

The muscles in Mike's face tensed. "So he let me grow up believing a lie."

"I know it's probably not the explanation you were looking for. He lied in case you ever came in contact with her."

Mike slumped over the Formica tabletop.

"I'm struggling to relate to any of this. I just feel angry about the whole damn thing," he mumbled.

"That accident," said Mrs. Kohl as she chewed a small bite of bread, "happened to all of us, not just your sister. My husband and I didn't keep the truth from our Scotty. He grew up knowing he threw that brick."

"Oh!" Jennifer involuntarily put her right hand on her chest.

"We should have protected him. We should have lied. But we didn't. So Scotty grew up knowing what he did. Later, he became a bitter young man. He was killed in a bar fight. My husband and I divorced nine years ago, after Scotty was killed. Scotty was twenty-four when he was stabbed."

Gradually Mike said, "I'm sorry that happened to you. You're right. I didn't mean to be selfish. Maybe I shouldn't have come here and dragged all this up."

"Don't be silly, Michael." Mrs. Kohl gave Jennifer a knowing look. "It was time for all this to come out. Time for you to move on. I've moved on, as hard as it was to do so. Life is a gift to be enjoyed. I'm just glad I didn't kick the bucket before you found me."

Mike and Jenifer laughed. Suddenly Mike was struck with a thought. "Do you have any photos of her?"

"Your sister?"

"No, my mother."

"You bet I do. I got a shoebox filled with old photos." Mrs. Kohl got up and disappeared down the hallway.

Mike leaned into Jennifer and whispered. "That brick could have landed on *my* head. Or I might have thrown it. I might have been the one to kill my sister."

"Shhh, here she comes."

Mrs. Kohl set a small box on the table and sat down. "Me and your mother were close at one point," she said. "Best friends. That's why I have so many photos of your family." She rifled through the contents then pushed the box aside and gave Mike a small stack of photos. Riley was in the first photo. She was using a swing set in some park. Huge smile. Small hands tightly gripping the chains. There were words on the back of the photo: Riley—Age 5. Mike passed the photo to Jennifer. The next photo showed Riley blowing out four candles atop a chocolate cake. Behind her was a young woman. The woman was bent forward over Riley's head. Her cheeks were puffed out as if she too was blowing out the candles.

Mike's face went white. "That woman is my mother?"

"Sure is. Always liked that particular photograph."

"Do you know where she went to?"

"Michael, I don't have a clue. She just up and left without a word to anyone."

Mike stood up. "We've got to be going," he said. "Do you mind if I keep these photos. I'd like to take my time and give them a good looking over in private."

"They're yours. Keep them or throw them away if they hurt too much."

Mrs. Kohl led the way to the entryway. On the front porch she gave Mike the box. He looked down at the array of color images. *There must be at least fifty.*

Mike said, "I can't tell you how much I appreciate your kindness, the trouble you went through for me. I'm sorry about what happen to Scotty. I'm sorry about your husband. I can't believe things like this happen to good people."

"Life doesn't play favorites," she said.

Jennifer hugged the old woman then they started down the walkway toward Mike's pickup. "Hey, Michael," Mrs. Kohl yelled as they reached the sidewalk. Mike and Jennifer turned and looked at her. She waved both hands above her head as she continued. "I like your pineapple shirt!" she laughed.

Mike waved to her. "Thanks," he said.

Then she said, "In that shirt you look just like your father. Your parents lived in Florida before taking those teaching jobs. He was always wearing those kind of shirts."

IN A MOMENT they were back in Mike's pickup. Mike behind the wheel staring at the birthday photo. Jennifer in the passenger seat, cardboard box across her lap. Mike tilted the photo to Jennifer. "This woman behind Riley," His voice quivered. "This woman. . ."

"Yes, your mother, she was pretty."

"This woman," he repeated, "this woman is Mrs. Stoll."

"Who?"

"Mrs. Stoll. The woman who rents me the backyard bungalow. The woman married to Captain Stoll. That's who."

At first, Jennifer did not believe the accusation. But Mike was adamant.

"My family," he said, "the big masquerade. And here's the kicker: for the past fifteen years, I've been living in my missing mother's backyard. Ha! For fifteen years I've been celebrating holidays, birthdays, going on outings and to the shopping center with her. All the while helping her husband, or whoever he is, with his business. My God, you can't make up shit like this."

They sat in silence, each with their own thoughts.

Jennifer said, "I want to be supportive; I want to help."

"I'm not asking for sympathy."

"I just want to help."

"I can't get my brain around any of this."

"Okay. I'm going to start helping right now. Trade places with me."

"What?"

"Trade places, you can't drive in this state of mind. And we have to get going to the hospital right now."

He opened his mouth, ready to say something. Then closed it and opened the door.

Jennifer walked around the pickup, got in and started up the motor, which sputtered for a moment before settling into a low rumble.

When they got to the hospital's first floor reception area the young woman named Cassidy directed them to a cubical-like room near the cafeteria. With an outstretched hand, Cassidy indicated the vinyl couch. Mike and Jennifer sat down. Cassidy told them about the event, about how Pops collapsed in the middle of an aisle at Ace Hardware. He was unconscious when the paramedics arrived, breathing erratically and shallow. In transit to the emergency room, he had several strokes. His heart gave out while he was on the table.

Then there were forms to fill out. It was a good thing Jennifer brought the mortuary information. Mike gave Cassidy the business card that was in the envelope. "Oh, yes," she said, "I know Bill Williams. He's a real nice person. You two will get along just fine." As she talked, Mike's attention flitted around the room. White walls. No wall hangings. People were sobbing in the adjacent room.

Cassidy gave Mike a plastic bag stuffed with Pops's belongings, the clothes he had been wearing at Ace. She also gave him a practical advice booklet containing issues about end of life: the bereavement process and support groups, obtaining the medical certificate, registering the death, arranging the funeral. Cassidy touched Mike's hand, the one gripping the booklet. "To reduce the risk of identity theft, notifications should be promptly made. And you'll have to file a Tax Return for him also, but your attorney will go over all that with you. Do you have an attorney?" "Yes." Mike placed the booklet under his arm, opened his wallet and retrieved a business card. "He sent this to me a while ago, after his ministroke," Mike said. "Oh, Mister Kirby. He's a nice person," she said. "You'll like him."

When the paperwork was completed, Cassidy told them to follow her to the bereavement room. She guided them down a hallway maze. They went past the Cardiac Care Unit. Mike could hear hospital workers talking in the area around the corner. Someone had had a heart attack and fallen off his roof. It was touch and go. Cassidy turned a corner and moved down an empty hallway. Over her shoulder she said, "Do you want a member of your religious community to join you?" "No," Mike muttered.

They rounded another corner and Cassidy stopped in front of a section where the hallway was lined with glass doors and floor to ceiling windows. Drapes hid the interior of each room.

Jennifer adjusted the blue butterfly hair clips that kept her bangs from her eyes. Her eyes were red, her nose stuffy.

Mike thanked Cassidy. She left.

Mike and Jennifer stood in front of the draped room. He wanted to go in but needed to wait a moment. He sensed Jennifer next to him, moving closer. Then she took his hand in hers. *How many more years do we have together?* His thoughts went to the inside of the room. Pops would be in there, head sticking out from under a sheet draped over him. No longer would he be in his 501s and white T-shirt and steel-toed boots. He would be as naked as when he entered the world. But now his hair would be gray and the top digit of his left forefinger would be missing and his eyes would be yellowy from cataracts he refused to deal with.

"You ready to go in?" Jennifer asked.

Mike sighed, took his time answering. *Just relax. I've got to relax. These things happen.* But he wasn't quite ready for the anguish, wasn't quite ready to accept the finality of it all.

"Not just yet," he said, squeezing her hand.

He gave Jennifer the booklet, suddenly, and reaching into his back pocket retrieved his phone. No longer did he have control over his actions. His brain was on autopilot as he selected a telephone number. And while the connection went through, he chewed the inside of his cheek, ignoring the pain and the slight taste of blood.

A woman answered. He recognized the voice, soft, kind sounding. His voice quivered. "Mom?"

Past the verbal silence, Mike could hear birds chirping away from that distant location. *She must be on the back patio. Maybe sitting in the wrought iron chair next to the koi pond, relaxing.* She had a fascination with watching the single red koi as it swam beneath the maze of water lilies, separating itself from its brethren of beautiful blues, yellows, golds and greens, seeking to hide from outsider scrutiny.

He did not ask again. He did not want to overwhelm her.

After an agonizing moment the woman spoke. "Yes." she said.

About the Author

Ron D'Alena was born in San Francisco and earned an MBA at the University of San Francisco. He worked for several Bay Area technology research companies followed by a stint at Cisco Systems before moving to Southern Oregon. He now enjoys an outdoor lifestyle, guitar hacking, his family and writing. Over the years, his short stories have appeared in numerous journals and magazines.

Made in United States
North Haven, CT
29 February 2024

49374475R00104